Victoria Villas

A novella by Alistair Wilkinson

TEXT COPYRIGHT: ALISTAIR WILKINSON

FRONT COVER ILLUSTRATION COPYRIGHT: CHRIS LILLYWHITE

Also by Alistair Wilkinson:

Suspended

The Balance

Stella the Zombie Killer Volume One (illustrated by Alison Rasmussen)

Stella the Zombie Killer Volume Two (illustrated by Alison Rasmussen)

Stella the Zombie Killer Volume Three (illustrated by Alison Rasmussen)

Stella the Zombie Killer Volume Four (illustrated by Alison Rasmussen)

Of Deads

For the latest news on Alistair Wilkinson's writing email alistairwilkinsonauthor@gmailcom

Or find Alistair Wilkinson Author on Facebook or tweet @algy04.

For my boys and for the games they played and the games to come.

Victoria Villas

It was the smell. He couldn't remember ever not smelling it. Age. Something old, too old. Something like that one time when a pig had died in the summer and no one had noticed for a whole day. The grown-ups had blamed the flies for that. There were no flies, not since the crash, and how were they supposed to notice a new, fouler smell mixed in with the older, already-foul smell, if there were no flies to warn them with their tell-tale buzz? By the time it was noticed, it was because it was the worst. The worst for that week, anyway. The smell was worse in the summer, worse in the autumn winds, worse in spring after a cold winter of disinfectant. For years it had got worse and worse; through the year-long night, that distant memory that Sean wouldn't even remember now; through the rains, the downpours, the monsoons that came after; through the long hot summers when the sun first shone again; through the winds and the ice and the thaw; a smell so bad Michael often didn't even notice it anymore. Until it was gone.

'Straight home, Michael,' Mrs Lansdown said. She was pegging out washing. It would dry overnight in the July heat.

She was right; it was nearly dark, the yards all plunged in shade as the summer sun sank below the buildings, and Michael's father had always insisted they return before dark. But Sean was nowhere to be seen.

'I haven't seen him,' Mrs Lansdown said, sensing his question.

Michael looked around; he was surrounded by the dark brick of the back-to-back terraced housing of Victoria Villas. Two long rows of back-bedroom windows stretched away on either side, one side dark, the other flashing in the light from the sinking sun. Two long rows of monochrome solar-panelled rooftops, the ice-smooth sheets only broken by the occasional dormer built in the time before. Two long rows of garden walls and fences, each kept at the required 1.3 metres. Michael imagined that he stood between two huge lengths of train carriages, stuck on a middle platform in a station waiting for a non-existent guard to come tell hm to move.

At one end more houses cut across and terminated the lines, at the other a huge brick wall, twenty metres high, old brick, dark brick, two small windows right under the eaves, a warehouse. Sean's favourite place.

'Straight home, Michael,' Mrs Lansdown said again. 'You know how your father gets.'

Michael turned from the warehouse wall, trudged to the alleyway that separated the rows of yards in Victoria Villas, and dawdled back to their house. He wanted to go look for Sean, make sure he knew it was time to come home, but Sean knew their father would not accept lateness. Only an angel can be late, he always said. Only an angel can be out after dark.

The angels. The protectors from before the long night. Last week, there had seen one in their narrow strip of sky. The birdsong alarm, then the noise of their jetpack, the weak contrail, a streak across the blue sky. Stay still. That's what their father, and Mrs Lansdown and all the other adults,

5

always said. If you hear the birdsong or see an angel in the sky, stay still, wait for the all clear.

That's it, Michael thought.

He turned and hurried along the alley, ducking past Mrs Lansdown's yard and onto the warehouse wall. At the passage end there was a door. Michael was sure it had once been locked. Two summers ago he and Sean had found it open. Mr Maher, the electrician, had been working in there, linking the many solar panels on the warehouse's vast roof to the power supply of the rest of Victoria Villas. The last two winters had been comfortable, every house was warm and lit, every stove worked whenever it was needed. Vegetables grown in the yards where the walls and fences had been removed, where the small lawns and patios had been dug over, planted, harvested, the crops blanched and then frozen, the solar power ensuring they stayed frozen.

And the meat from the pigs and chickens. Whole houses at one end of Victoria Villas were dedicated to livestock: pigs on the ground floors, chickens on the first floors. Their meat could be frozen too. Mr Gaska was the butcher. He had helped others learn too. Michael's father had told him that he should decide soon what he wanted to do; electrician, butcher, plumber, builder, roofer, outsider, all were part of the community in Victoria Villas. His job now, his and Sean's and three other children, was to feed the pigs and chickens, keep the sties and runs clean, fetch the eggs, report illnesses to Michael's father, the veterinarian. Michael was never told that he might also be a veterinarian; that was for Sean. Michael would be jealous except he knew that Sean hated the idea; he couldn't stand to see the suffering of animals. The sounds, the smells, they haunted him in his dreams, woke him at night, sweating and gasping. Michael could hear him. At first, he'd gone to him, comforted him, tried to tell him it would be okay, but Sean said he was too old for that now. He was ten, two years younger than Michael.

Michael stepped to the door, pushed it open just enough to squeeze through, and closed it again behind him. Sean loved the warehouse. It was soft and calm, the hard edges and echoes of Victoria Villas ended as soon as soon as the door was closed again.

Carpets. A carpet warehouse. Carpets in huge rolls, on horizontal bars racked high against the walls and in the middle aisles, more were leaned against the walls and into the corners to stand against each other, like pillars from old Roman villas gathered together for warmth in the shadows. Rugs in huge piles. Mats, cut-offs and floor tiles, all soft, all piled. In the winter the smell of damp could become overpowering, but now, in the summer, it was soft and warm, a cocoon, a nest, a comfort, the smell simply a part of the inside and a comfort compared with that smell outside.

It was dark inside the warehouse; the only light coming from those small, dirty windows at the top of the wall and a pair of sky lights either side of the roof so far away.

Sean lolled on a red carpet, the softest they had found and his favourite. His small body easily balanced on top, legs and arms hanging either side of the roll, his longish hair, overdue for a cut, flopping over his face. Michael knew that his arms had tanned in the summer sun, but here in this dark, soft room he looked pale.

'Sean?' Michael whispered. No one had ever seen them in the warehouse, so he didn't know why he whispered. Sean didn't move. Asleep again. Michael walked purposefully to his brother and shook his shoulder.

'I'm awake,' said Sean. He moved his face just enough for his brother to see that his eyes were open. He smiled that charming smile of his.

'C'mon,' Michael moaned. 'Dad'll be angry if we don't get back soon.'

Sean shifted himself onto his back, cocking one leg over the other and staring up at the distant sky lights and the fading blue. 'He'll already be angry,' he said.

'Come on!'

'Okay, okay.'

Michael, dancing on the balls of his feet with nerves, dragged Sean off the wide roll of carpet and ushered him towards the warehouse door.

'Wait,' said Sean. 'We need to say goodbye.'

'There isn't time!' Michael cried. He tried to get a firmer grip on Sean's shoulders.

But Sean slipped out of his brother's grasp and dashed to the other side of the warehouse and a tall, wide steel shutter. Sean skidded to a halt, reached out his hand the metal. It was cold to the touch.

Michael grabbed again at his shoulder, pulling him away from the shutter. 'We need to go!' he hissed.

'Wait!' Sean struggled away from his brother and laid both hands flat against the ribbed metal. 'Hey!' he whispered into the shutter. 'Are you there?'

A sound from the other side of the shutter, a soft scraping, as if a paw were dabbing against the surface. Sean giggled and tapped in reply, a flutter of his fingers against the surface. As always, the movements on the other side increased, the pawing intensifying. To Sean, it was an excited sound, a friendly communication. To Michael, it was agitated, desperate.

'Are you okay?' Sean whispered. His hands were still on the shutter, feeling the scraping that was his only reply. Michael grabbed at his brother again, pulling at him to leave. Sean leaned his face closer to the metal. 'See you tomorrow.' Finally, he allowed his brother to pull him away and the two boys dashed through the warehouse, out into the alleyway, between the yards, towards the end and the smell of the pigs, the smell that, just as it started to compete with the other, older smell, made the other smell all the more noticeable, like it had waited all day just for the boys to compare it with the pigs'.

'Where have you been?' their father demanded. He was a tall man, tall and wide. Imposing, was the word. Ms Scott had taught that word in class last week, and Michael had pictured their father immediately. He'd looked over at Sean, and the two brothers had exchanged knowing nods.

'There was an angel,' Michael stammered. He always stammered when he spoke to their father.

'We stayed still,' Sean added. No stammer. Michael often envied him his confidence. His younger brother was the one who could talk, the one who could smile naturally, confidently, reassuringly. He didn't smile now; not the time, the boy knew. Sean's face was solemn, apologetic with just a touch of c'est la vie.

Their father glowered over them, his nostrils flaring, his breath rushing into his thick moustache, his eyes wide, searching Sean's face. He switched to Michael, who quailed under the glare. 'There was no angel,' he said, no hint of a question in his voice. 'There was no birdsong.' Michael cursed himself; if any angel was sighted the alarm was raised. Birdsong. And there were always two watchers, one in the roof spaces of each side of the Villas. 'No angel,' their father continued, 'just two boys who cannot understand a curfew.'

The front room of their house was dark; the windows were boarded up, the door blocked and barred, as they had been since the depths of the long night. Sometimes, Michael fancied he could remember them from before, remember their light, the sunshine... It couldn't be true; there was no sunshine for a year after the crash. And Victoria Villas had not been their home before the crash. Now, all the front rooms were like this: windows and doors boarded and barred, locked, the world outside, the streets, kept hidden. Their father's back was to the boarded window, his face red in what little light filtered through from the kitchen. 'It's important that you know not to lie about things like this. Those things will kill you, do you understand? They will see you move and their lasers will find you and cut you and burn you. And they will bring the monsters that live in the world. The world is full of monsters. Your mother...' He stopped, sucked up a great intake of air through his nose. His elbows crooked, fists clenched at his hips. He stepped past the boys, knocking them just a little, just enough to show his impatience, and pushed the door closed, leaving the room black.

Their mother. Michael's memories of her were clear and vague at the same time. She was like those scenes he'd seen of flashbacks on the DVDs that they played every week. Some whole scenes but mostly bits of extracts: long hair that swung near him and tickled his nose, a familiar, comforting smell, the touch of a soft hand. Softness. That was the memory of his mother. Sean would never talk about their mother. Michael assumed he couldn't remember her.

He sat in the yard on the following morning, feeling the sun on his bare arms and trying to ignore Mrs Lansdown's sympathetic looks. Sean slumped against the fence, curled into the shade. The pigs and chickens were fed, the eggs collected. The two boys would have to clean the sties and coop that afternoon.

'Lunch time soon,' Mrs Lansdown called over the fence. 'I've got a lovely piece of chicken pie that Mr Lansdown didn't fancy last night if you want it.'

Sean lifted his head. Mrs Lansdown was the best cook in the Villas. Michael could see that his head was suddenly filled with gravy.

'Mashed potato too,' she continued. 'No butter, of course.' She laughed. Michael knew that it was forced. 'I miss butter.' Her voice broke a little, almost imperceptibly, but Michael heard it. Mrs Lansdown had always talked. Too much, their father often said. Something was wrong but

Michael had no idea how to ask, could feel his stammer bocking him before he'd even tried to say anything.

'You okay, Mrs L?' Sean called out from the shadow of the fence.

'I'm fine, thanks, Sean,' Mrs Lansdown called back, the usual pleasure at speaking to the boys back in her voice.

'And how's Mr L?'

'Oh, he's great, thanks,' Mrs Lansdown answered in a sing-song voice. 'He was back on his feet this morning. He's as right as rain.'

'Have you got any gravy to go with the pie?' Sean asked.

'I certainly have.'

Sean scrabbled to his feet, wincing a little as he moved. He pulled himself up to peek over the fence and smiled at Mrs Lansdown. 'I'd love a piece of pie, please.' He looked down at his brother. 'And so would Michael.'

Later that day, the sties and coop cleaned and the boys' bellies full of pie and gravy, the brothers played in the back alley of the Villas. There were other children, some older, some younger, who all played every afternoon.

There were two games. First, they had time trials, sprints up and down the alley. The older children always won but Michael was getting closer to their times. Sean liked to operate the stopwatch on the one phone that the grown-ups let them use each afternoon. He liked to run but he would get jealous of the older boys' longer strides and give up after the first attempt. Still, he had to do four lengths, the same as everybody else. Exercise and fitness, they were told, were important. It was important to be strong, fit and alert.

Stamina and speed from the time trials. Sharpness from the Grabber Game.

It had to be the afternoon when the sun would be in the face of the runner and so the grabbers couldn't use shadows to help them. The game had been invented for them by the adults and it was simple: each child took a turn at being the runner and had to get from one end of the alley to the other without being grabbed. Each of the other children had to have their back to the runner and had to stay still – any turning or peeking meant disqualification and they had to miss their next turn – until they could see the runner, then they were allowed one step to see if they could grab the runner. The grabber would try to take a noisy step to alert the next child that the runner was coming, but that was the only noise they were allowed to make. After the grab attempt they could then shuffle forward, taking the smallest steps, the heel of one foot having to touch the toes of the other. The alley was narrow, only about a metre and a half, so it was really hard to do, and hardly any runner ever managed it, so the scoring was done on how many children could be passed safely. On this day there were seven children, so the maximum score was six. The children enjoyed the game and the competition was fierce. Echoes of hissed whispers – the children were not allowed to shout – bounced around the hot alley: 'You're dead!'

Michael had scored four. The other children between one and three. Even though he was getting bigger and it was harder and harder to squeeze past the grabbers, he was the best at the game and had been for six months since an older girl, who had always scored at least three, was

13

taken to join the grown-ups and given a special job; she was an outsider now.

Sean was the last child to try. Michael, the final grabber, watched his brother as he stood at one end of the hot, dusty alley. It was 100 metres to the finish line, the door to the warehouse. The other children, his fellow grabbers, all turned their backs to Sean, not knowing when he would start. The sun was still high in the sky, pressing its heat into this tight space, making the children sweat. The alley's dust stuck to their skin, making them wipe at their arms and faces, leaving dirty streaks across tanned flesh. Michael knew that Sean liked this part the best, the quiet anticipation as he teased the grabbers. Sean had spoken of it many times in the carpet warehouse, sharing his tactics with the thing on the other side of the shutter. He could see the shoulders of the first of them, tense and square, their hands at their sides curling and uncurling into fists, their arms moving in and out, feeling for the runner, knowing he will come but their anticipation was nothing like Sean's. Theirs was the unknown, like standing on the edge of a precipice waiting to fall. Being the first grabber was the worst role in the game; it was so easy to get past them and then they were out. Sean hated it. Michael always said he didn't mind. Sometimes, Sean would tell Michael that he didn't want things enough. Michael would listen and smile down at his younger brother.

Michael imagined Sean as he walked easily up to the first grabber, paused behind them, enjoyed for a moment the feeling of control, then slipped past, the grabber flailing as they stumbled their one step, and then, as often happened with the first grabber, taking another half step to regain their balance. Sean smiled. The first grabber had to go and sit down.

The second, just a few metres away, tensed, ready to grab. Sean scuttled forward, scuffed at the wall to his left and then darted right, passing the grabber and running the next few metres in just a couple of seconds. This grabber also stumbled as it tried to readjust, and they took a second and then third step. Another smirk from Sean and another grabber had to sit on the floor.

The third was ready, had set themself to the left, leaving a clear space to the right. Sean couldn't use the same trick again. He smiled, trusting his speed. He flew past, his shoulder scraping the right wall, making him stumble and scrape his shoes along the path, his feet slapping into the concrete to regain his balance. The grabber missed, but retained their balance and began their slow, tiny-stepped pursuit.

The fourth was further away, at least ten metres, but fully alert, and the third was right behind, coming at Sean, their arms raised, ready to grab. Dancing on the balls of his feet, Sean hesitated, swinging his head from the approaching grabber and to the back of the fourth. It was in the middle of the alley, so the distraction could work again. He went for it, this time scuffing the right wall and darting left, ducking as he did so. The arm of the grabber swept across his hair, making him duck further and stumble into the wall, crashing his elbow into the bricks to try and keep his balance but only managing to throw himself the other way and fall into the middle of the alley, scraping his knee and drawing blood.

Sean gritted his teeth as he rolled over and sprang back to his feet, two grabbers now in their slow but inevitable pursuit.

The fifth waited and listened to the shuffling steps of the other grabbers. They would try to tell when Sean might try to get past by raising the noise of their scraping feet. Sean ran on, watching for loose stones on the ground, his steps silent, closing on the fifth, knowing he couldn't wait too long. He stopped, listened to the grabber's excited breaths, watched as hands and arms moved, hovered, waited, rested, moved again. Sean kicked at the wall to his left, watched the grabber flinch, wait, relax again. Sean imagined the smug smile on the grabber's face. He took a half-step forward, the pursuers scuffing their feet, the grabber spreading their arms, their hands turned backwards, their fingers spread into hooks that swung at nothing. Sean stepped back, stepped forward again, scuffed at the wall, the grabber's arms shooting out again, the hooked fingers clawing at empty air again. Sean dropped silently to his hands and scuttled forwards. His pursuers' scrapings louder than ever, the grabber swinging their arms frantically, windmilling at their sides, Sean practically crawling past, an involuntary gasp of frustration as they finally saw him on the ground and just as they took their one step he was back on his feet and running at the final grabber.

Michael waited for his brother, proud but nervous. When he'd been made the last grabber he'd been sure that Sean would make it this far. Michael listened to the shuffling mini steps of the other children, imagining Sean looking over his shoulder at the chasing grabbers. There would only be three of them at the most, but those few children would fill the alleyway and seem like a horde of monsters closing in, their arms and fingers outstretched, reaching, grasping, clawing. They made the runner make mistakes. Michael spread his feet a little further apart, kept his arms still, his hands loose, ignored the sweat on his palms, readied himself for Sean's attempt to finish the game. He listened intently, straining his ears to hear his brother's steps. Nothing. He tried to stay calm, to not let his breathing become too fast and drown out any tell-tale noises of movement behind him. He listened.

Birdsong.

Somehow, he made himself even stiller, his already frozen limbs turning to stone while his heart suddenly hammered in his chest, seemed to rise through his neck and into his head, thudding against the inside of his skull. The heat trapped in the alley suddenly seemed too much, as if it would wrap itself around him, a snake ready to squeeze and twist itself into his body, crush his chest, stop him from breathing.

In the distance, a noise. Jetpack. An angel. He couldn't tell how high, didn't dare look up even though he knew it wouldn't be directly over the Villas yet. Their father's words about hot lasers ran through his mind. He saw flesh sliced and dissolving, puddling and steaming in the heat of the alleyway. He saw his mother's long hair falling, her smell drifting away in an unfelt wind, the touch of her hands gone. In the brick and concrete of the alley, all softness was gone, leaving just this hard fear that promised a short, hard life of emptiness, a void that had no touch, no smell, no love.

Sean! His brother came to his mind, forced his hammering heart back down into his chest, lifted the heavy heat. Where was he? Right behind, waiting to make his move, to win the game? He wouldn't. Michael told himself over and over that his brother would not move, that he would not use the grabbers' enforced stillness just to win a game. But Michael knew that he could not guess his brother's actions. He knew that later, if they were still alive, he would sneak into the warehouse and loll on the rolls of carpet, then slip away to the shutter and whisper the stories of the day, but he had no idea what Sean thought about, why he went into places he was not supposed to go, why or how he could speak to adults so easily, so comfortably, yet be so quiet, so reserved, so distant. Michael suddenly felt like he didn't know Sean, not like he should, not like brothers should.

He listened for sounds from the other grabbers, any hint that Sean might be moving. Nothing. He longed to turn his head, to look at his brother and know what he was doing, to tell him to think of what their father would say, would do if he moved during the alarm. His fear of their father was a physical thing that towered over him, controlled him, but it was a thing that didn't seem to follow Sean in the same way. As he so often did, Michael tried to project his fear onto his brother, tried to send it behind him, tried to smother his brother's impulses.

The jetpack was closer now; it would soon be above them, able to see them if they moved. They had learned about hawks and how they could see mice from high in the sky. How high? Michael couldn't remember. Hundreds of metres? Miles? No, not miles. But hundreds of metres, yes, definitely. A mouse. His head was bigger than a mouse, much bigger.

The noise of the jetpack was right over Michael now. He could feel the angel adding its weight to the heat, pressing down on him, waiting for him to move. He was the runner now and the grabber was deadly. He tried to ignore his fear, to focus instead on Sean; he strained to listen, to try to hear anything except the angel's jetpack.

The angel passed overhead, higher than Michael had first thought, although that could be wishful thinking, he knew. How long since the birdsong alarm? Minutes? Hours? Surely not seconds? Surely it was nearly over. A bead of sweat fell into his eye. He flinched, just a little, and tried to blink his eyes clear.

A scrape on the ground behind him, a shoe on the dusty path, scraping to get ready to move, shifting because of cramp, stumbling after holding an awkward balance for so long. Michael didn't know. He could only hold himself still and hope.

Another scrape, this time louder, longer, a boy getting his feet into a more comfortable position, the cramp in his legs unbearable. That must be it.

Michael waited. No more noise, no more scraping, no running from the runner.

The noise of the jetpack didn't change, didn't get any closer, didn't alter course at all, and it moved away, beyond the Villas.

Birdsong.

Michael sighed and sagged with relief.

Sean dashed past him, ran on and slapped the door to the warehouse. He turned and grinned triumphantly at his brother. The other grabbers all stood stunned, while adults peered over fences and out of windows, some smiling, some giving a thumbs up, either to all the children for their steadfastness during the alarm, or to Sean for his audacity to win the game, Michael never knew.

Later that evening, Michael found Sean in the warehouse. He had expected to find him lying on a roll of carpet staring up at the bright skylight, but his brother was at the shutters, his hands and cheek on the metal.

'What are you doing?' Michael asked.

Sean was startled; he hadn't heard Michael arrive, was lost in some daydream. He turned his face away from his brother and Michael was sure he saw the glint of tears on his cheeks.

'Are you okay?' Michael asked.

Sean nodded, his short hair rubbing against the shutter. 'I was telling her about today.'

'Who?'

Sean nodded into the shutter, causing quiet creaks and rattles. Whatever was on the other side scrabbled in return, its hands pawing at the shutter. Michael had never heard Sean refer to whatever it was as 'her' before.

'She likes to hear about my day,' Sean said. His voice was muffled, whispered into the shutter, but Michael could hear it well enough.

'Who?' he asked again.

20

Sean turned to his brother. 'Mum,' he said.

Michael stood over his brother, unable to move or speak. It was like he was still in the game, still waiting to grab, still waiting for Sean to make his move, to do whatever it was he was planning to do. The moment stretched, became a long pause, Michael frozen, Sean on his knees leaning his head against the shutter.

'Mum's dead,' said Michael.

Sean looked up at his brother and smiled. 'No, she's not.'

Michael stammered as he tried to speak, gave up, stood and waited. Finally, he sighed, 'We need to go,' Michael insisted. 'Dad will be getting impatient.'

Sean nodded. Michael knew he would come; he was never late two nights in a row.

They made their way home, Sean smiling proudly as they moved along the alley. Mrs Lansdown wasn't in her yard and all the other children were gone. There would be an adult or two or three watching from back-bedroom windows, but for this moment they felt alone. Michael felt the isolation of carrying a secret, every echoing footstep a reminder of his brother's delusion.

They had the house to themselves that night; their father was at a meeting of all the adults. They had met three nights ago but now they had to meet again. Something important, their father had said, before leaving.

'Let me show you something,' said Sean. He led Michael to their father's study,

'We're not supposed to go in there,' said Michael.

'It's okay. I've been in before. He never knows.'

Michael allowed himself to be led into the room. He'd never been in their father's study except to be lectured about something: being the older brother, looking out for Sean, taking responsibility, for pigs, for chickens, for vegetables, for silence, for watching the sky, for being still when the birdsong sounded, for complaining about the smell, for crying when he was in pain, for crying when he missed his mother, for crying when he just felt like crying.

It was dark. None of the front rooms, as the adults called them, had sunlight because of the boarded windows. Sean switched on the electric light, the illumination from the bare bulb immediate and harsh. The Villas was Michael's and Sean's world; it was hard to imagine anything beyond the slate-grey and solar-panel silver of the Villas' roofs. Perhaps there was nothing. Perhaps this was it, the Villas and Sean and father and Mrs Lansdown and the other children and adults. And the angels that kept them prisoner. Michael paused at that thought; he'd never considered himself a prisoner before. The Villas provided everything he needed. He looked over at the boarded window and wanted to know what was on the other side. In school they had learned about streets and cities, about how unsafe they were. That danger was on the other side of the board. He took a step closer, but Sean grabbed at his arm.

'Over here,' said the younger brother. He dragged Michael to the desk, showed him piles of scribbled papers. They were minutes of the meetings in which the adults had made decisions about pigs and chickens and growing vegetables and keeping watch for angels and laundry and rationing the homebrew.

'What's homebrew?' Sean asked.

'Alcohol,' said Michael. 'Dad drinks it at night when we're in bed.'

'That's poison,' said Sean.

Michael nodded. 'But the adults like it.' He remembered seeing Mr Lansdown drink some homebrew one afternoon. The man had ignored Mrs Lansdown's complaints about it not being the right time to drink. He's grimaced as he drank it, like Sean when he was forced to eat a Brussels' sprout, but unlike Sean, he'd carried on, taking more and more, grimacing, but still drinking. 'Well, maybe they don't like it, but they seem to enjoy it.'

'Dad likes it,' said Sean. Michael nodded his agreement. 'He doesn't seem to have it rationed either.'

'He has a thing with Mr Ellis: extra eggs for extra homebrew.'

'That's cheating. How do they get away with it?'

'I think there are lots of little agreements like that.'

'It doesn't seem fair.'

Michael shook his head in agreement. 'Never mind. What else did you want to show me?'

Sean sifted through the papers, moved a large bunch of keys to one side and pulled out their father's laptop. 'He doesn't lock it. Doesn't have a password or anything.' It was silver and shined in the hash light from the bare bulb, flashing white as Sean raised the screen into position. 'Look,' he said. Michael leaned over his brother; there was a paused video. It was hard to see properly as wherever it had been filmed was dark. The shot focused on a woman, her arms in the air, surrounded by other people, their arms similarly raised. Her hair was flailing around her head, shining in the bright lights that beamed onto the frozen people.

'What are they doing?' Michael asked.

'Dancing,' Sean replied. He hit play. The noise and movement were so sudden that Michael jumped and staggered back a half-step. The music was loud, a heavy beat thumping from the speakers. The woman was dancing, her movements smooth, energetic, fun. She was having fun. Her smile and flailing hair shined in the light. She beckoned to the camera, both hands calling them over. That hair. A halo. This was what angels were supposed to be like.

'It's Mum,' said Michael. Sean nodded. He didn't take his eyes off the screen.

'Dad watches this every night. He drinks poison and he watches this.'

'Turn it off,' said Michael.

Sean didn't move, just kept staring.

'It's from before,' said Michael, more insistent now. 'Turn it off.'

'No, it's not from before. Look.' Sean paused the video, switched the view to the video's file and showed his brother the date. Two months ago.

'That can't be right.'

'It is right. Computers always get the date right. That's what they've said in class, that's how we know the date and the day, and we know how long since the crash and when our birthdays and Christmas are. The computers know. That's what they say.'

'It can't be. Mum's been dead since the crash.'

'She's there.' Sean pointed at the screen. 'Two months ago.' He looked up into his brother's face. 'Now she's in the warehouse.'

Michael was shaking his head. 'No, it can't be.' He refused to believe, but he found his hand reaching out to the keyboard and he brought the video back to the screen and pressed play. They watched their mother dance and laugh and sing, the images shining back from their eyes.

Moments or minutes or hours later Michael forced himself to close the screen of the laptop, tried not to match Sean's sigh of disappointment.

'We should go to her,' said Sean.

'Tomorrow,' Michael agreed.

'Now,' said Sean.

Michael shook his head. 'We can't be out after dark. The angels can see us but we can't see them.'

'Dad will be coming back in the dark.'

Michael shook his head again. 'He'll come through the roof spaces, you know that.'

The two boys left the study, retreated to their bedroom, a back room with a window. They squeezed onto the windowsill and stared up into the clear night sky. Stars. Millions and millions of them.

'Why don't you want to help Dad with the animals?' Michael asked. He tried to keep the jealousy out of his voice, but knew that he sounded not right, not bitter but a little sour.

Sean looked at his brother. 'The blood. No matter what Dad does there's always blood. Animals' blood. On his hands, on their skin and their feathers, in their eyes.'

'But Dad keeps them healthy, saves their lives.'

'So that they can be killed. He keeps them alive so that they can go to Mr Gaska's knives. They know; I've seen their eyes. They're so black and deep and there's death in everything they look at, including me.'

Michael didn't know what to say to that. His brother was right; the animals were delivered to Mr Gaska's house alive and out came meat which was then portioned out to the other houses. Sean ate the meat. He had no choice.

They both turned back to the stars. Birdsong. Something moved across the stars, joining the dots. Despite Michael's protest, Sean opened the window and the two boys settled on the floor well back from the starlight that pattered onto the old carpet and listened as the noise of the jetpack made its way across the night sky.

The boys fed and cleaned the pigs and the chickens. Mrs Lansdown was not in her yard all day. The boys had nothing to eat; their father was busy with a sick sow. He'd wanted Sean to help him but the smaller brother had hidden from their father, dashing out without washing and leaving his breakfast to coat his teeth all day.

In the afternoon they played their games. In the time trials Michael came second, his grin of triumph as bright as the summer sun. For the grabber game, there were two more children and so the score maximum score was eight. Michael claimed a four and a three: grabbed by the fifth child and grabbed three children himself. Sean claimed a one and a zero, grabbed at the second and no grabs himself.

Michael had watched him as much as possible throughout the day. His brother was like this, always up and down, king of the alley one day, pauper the next. Focused then inattentive. Passionate then uncaring. Something was wrong. Michael felt it too. Their mother. All day he kept seeing her, her hair bouncing in the lights of the dance floor, her smile, her hands and fingers beckoning him closer. She was beautiful, so much more beautiful than even he remembered.

Because of Mrs Lansdown's absence the game was cut short and half the children sent to laundry duty. Michael and Sean were left with nothing to do and so they drifted to the warehouse, Michael lying on the soft, musty carpet roll and Sean going again to the shutter, leaning his head against the metal and whispering through the barrier. At first, Michael tried to listen but he quickly gave up, preferring instead to remember the video of his mother. He closed his eyes, let the memory of the music sound in his ears and moved cautiously forward to take her hands and dance.

He didn't know he had fallen asleep, awareness only coming when Sean was shaking him awake. 'Mike, it'll be dark soon. We have to go.'

Michael raised his head, the image of his mother fading into the heights of the warehouse roof, the fading blue seeping through the skylight. 'I'm coming,' he mumbled.

The two boys made their way home. Their father was waiting for them.

'I need you two to tell me the truth,' he said. He was impatient, the brothers could tell, even angry. Neither said anything, simply nodding to show that they would.

'Have you been in the study?'

Both brothers froze, unable to answer. Michael could feel his stammer rising in his throat, the fear forcing him to speak the truth, the stammer forcing the words back down. Sweat broke out on his forehead, tears leapt to his eyes. Their father studied his face, saw the tell-tale signs, seemed to lean towards him, his face and eyes looming over him. Michael could see the red of the veins on his eyeballs.

'It was me,' said Sean, he moved forward half a step, to try to put himself between their father and Michael, looking up into their father's grimacing face. 'It was me,' he said again. 'I was in there.'

The father stepped back, staring at his youngest, his frustration a heat radiating from him. He turned on Michael. 'You let your younger brother break the rules?' he demanded. 'You let him do as he likes? You let him go through my things? You let him into the study even though you know I have told you so many times that you are not to go in there?'

Sean stepped forward again, shouting up at their father. 'It was me, not Mike! Leave him alone. He didn't even know that I'd gone in there!'

The father pushed Sean aside and lunged at Michael, grabbing his shoulders and hauled him close till their faces were just centimetres apart. He began screaming into his eldest son's face. 'You watch your brother! You follow the rules! You don't know this world, the dangers it has! You must watch your brother!' He fell silent, breathing hard, his breath stinking of the home brew, the poison. Michael grimaced, tried not to breathe through his nose. Their father shook him hard, making his head snap back and forth, jarring his neck.

'Leave him alone!' Sean shouted. 'Leave him alone!'

Their father shook Michael again. The elder brother lost balance and his whole body whipped back and forth, his knees sagging, and finally giving way altogether. He fell, their father stumbling after him.

Their father yelled, 'You stupid boy!' as he tumbled forward. He didn't fall. He stood over his son, staring down at him. He seemed to think for a moment and then grabbed Michael, hauled him to his feet and dragged him up the stairs towards the study at the front of the house. 'You let your brother in here, you may as well see it for yourself. I'll show you the room. I'll show you the room!'

Sean was left alone in the kitchen, crying into the palms of his hands.

The summer days stretched even as they shortened. July dragged by, the smell of the pigs and the chickens sometimes but not always covering that other smell.

The brothers fed and cleaned the animals. They played the games, getting a little better all the time. A little better at moving quickly and suddenly. A little better at being silent.

They hadn't seen Mrs Lansdown in more than a week and so rarely ate in the middle of the day. Their visits to the warehouse shortened along with the days. Michael stayed on the carpets, Sean leant against the shutter, whispering and holding his hands against the metal, listening to the noises from the other side, calling whatever it was his mum.

One day, Michael went to his brother. 'It can't be Mum,' he said. He said it gently, as softly as he could and still be heard.

Sean shook his head, ignoring his brother.

'It can't be,' Michael said again. 'How is she alive? What does she eat? That's the world on the other side of the shutter. She couldn't survive in the world. No one can. Dad couldn't. Mr and Mrs Lansdown couldn't. None of the grownups could, that's why they're stuck in the Villas.' Sean turned away, refusing to listen. Michael reached for a name, someone to make his point. 'Stella!' he said. 'Stella Reeve, even she couldn't survive out there.'

Sean turned to his brother. 'Stella the Killer?' he asked. Michael nodded. 'She could,' said Sean. 'She would. She'd be the killer in the streets instead of the ring.'

Michael shook his head. 'No, not even Stella,' he insisted.

Sean turned back to the shutter. 'She could,' he mumbled.

Michael said nothing, just watched his brother lean his head against the shutter. There was no one to talk to, no one to help. All the grownups had their jobs that kept them busy all day, all the other children were kept busy too. Sean would be busier if he didn't hide from their father. Michael would be busier if their father thought that he could help more with the animals. The stammer lurked in his throat, stopping him from calling out to Sean. What could he say? What could he do for a little boy who wanted his mother so badly he thought that thing behind the shutters was their mother?

It took him several attempts, but finally he said again, 'It can't be her, Sean. Dad says there's monsters in the world.'

'Mum's not a monster,' said Sean.
'Mum's dead.'
'How do you know?'
'Dad said.'
'Exactly.'

Michael had never considered not believing their father. He was impatient and angry but that was because of the angels and the monsters and the upkeep of the Villas. This was all they had, and their father did everything he could to protect that. That was what he'd always said, what all the grownups said. Ms Scott said it in class. They learned about reading and writing and maths. Ms Scott brought in guest speakers, just the other grownups from the Villas, and they learned how to plumb and build and mend. They learned about electricity and solar panels and soil nutrients. They learned about first aid and controlling infections. They learnt that if anyone died that they mustn't go near the body, that they should get a grownup, get them quick. Never, they were told, be alone with a dead body.

'There's something wrong here,' said Michael. Sean turned to him. 'Here at the Villas. It's not right.'

'What do you mean?' Sean asked.
'We're not kids, not like the ones in the DVDs.'
'That's because of the angels.'
'But how did it happen?'

'Because of the crash.'

Michael nodded. 'I know, but there was nothing that night. Nothing happened to us. It was just stuff on the telly. Do you remember?' Sean shook his head. 'We were watching the Games, Stella was playing, remember?' Sean shook his head again. 'You were too young. We were watching and the TV switched over to the news on its own. Mum had told Dad off. He said it wasn't him.' Michael stopped. 'No, that wasn't it. It didn't change channel. It was just that the news came on instead of the Games.'

'The Cynosure Games?' Sean asked. They had both enjoyed watching DVDs of Stella's highlights. They had pretended to be her when they played their own games in the alley. She was so fast, so strong. She would never be grabbed. Sometimes, Michael felt like that in the game, like he couldn't be stopped, like he just knew which way the grabber would go and he could slip safely by. It was the only time in his life that he felt powerful and strong.

Michael nodded again. 'The TV screen had split in four a few times that night, each corner had a spaceship. You remember the spaceships?'

Sean frowned, unsure. 'Sort of,' he said.

'They were blown up. Right there on the TV. Blinding white explosions. And the world ended that night. That was when the monsters came.'

'Did you see them?'

'No. Dad took us up to bed. He told us, told me, I suppose, because you were so little, that everything was going to be alright, that we shouldn't worry and we should just go to sleep. He said we were his strong little men.'

Michael paused, dazed for a moment by the memory of their father's kind and gentle words. 'He said that everything would be okay in the morning. He promised.'

Sean's cynicism twisted his face. 'He lied.'

The two boys fell silent, the rolls of carpet layering silence into the warehouse. They never saw their mother again. Their father said she died on that night, the first night. He told them that she hadn't known about the monsters, that no one had known, including him. She had tried to help someone. But they were a monster and they'd attacked her.

'What happened to Mum?' Sean asked.

'She died. The monsters got her.'

'That's what Dad says.'

'What do you mean?'

'He lied on that night and he's lying now,' said Sean. Michael was shaking his head, trying to speak, but his stammer stopped him. 'She's not dead. She's here.' Sean put his hand on the shutter. 'We have to open it.'

'No!' The word fell from Michael's mouth in a hissed whisper. 'It's not true, Sean. It can't be. Dad wouldn't lie about that.'

'He would.'

Michael waited for his brother to continue but Sean fell silent again, their father's dishonesty stopping his mouth.

Eventually, Sean spoke. 'We have to let her out,' he said. 'It's not fair that she's stuck in there.'

'It's not her. It can't be.'

'It must be. If it was a monster, why would the grown-ups keep it here?'

'Maybe they don't know about it. No one comes in here, just us. Or maybe it came since the last time anyone checked what was on the other side of the shutter.'

'Or maybe it's Mum. Maybe it's Mum and she wants to come to us. Maybe she's out there all alone surrounded by monsters and she needs our help!'

Her long hair, her smell, her touch. Michael remembered it all so clearly now. He wanted to feel her hair against his nose, smell her, touch her. He wanted it so badly.

'How would we open it?' Michael asked.

'The controls are at the side,' Sean replied.

The boys moved to the side of the shutter. A steel box on the wall, two buttons, one for up and one for down.

'It's easy,' said Sean. 'Press it.'

Michael lifted his hand then hesitated. 'It will be noisy,' he said. 'The grown-ups will come. Maybe Dad...' His voiced trailed away.

Sean was excited, gabbling quickly. 'Dad will be pleased! You saw the video; he misses her!'

Michael's hand moved again, his finger resting on the up button.

'Push it!'

He pressed. Both boys held their breath. Nothing happened.

'What's wrong?' Sean asked.

'I don't know.' Michael released the button, pressed again. Nothing. 'Maybe it's the power?' Michael was guessing and he knew it.

'What do we do?'

'I don't know.' Michael stared at the steel box.

'What's this?' Sean pointed to another smaller box. It had a lid, which Michael opened. There was a keyhole inside. 'Who would have the key?'

'Dad,' said Michael. 'Dad would have it.' The two boys looked at each other and remembered the bunch of keys in the study. 'Tonight,' said Michael. Sean nodded.

They left the warehouse and found their father standing in the alley.

'Home!' he hissed.

The brothers trailed behind their father, not daring to look at each other, the hopes of moments before falling into the dusty path. The sun was behind the rooftops of the Villas, the windows were all dark, lifeless. The Villas could have been empty but the boys knew that those windows would be filled with eyes. No one would say anything. All Mrs Lansdown had ever said was that they knew what their father was like. Everyone knew. No one said anything. What else happened behind those blank and boarded windows?

Inside their house their father turned on them, his face reddening. 'So, you think you're okay to go where you like, do as you like?' The two boys tried to say no but he spoke over them, looking from boy to the other, catching each of them in the fire of his eyes. 'You go where you've been told not to, you hide when there's work to be done.' He spoke directly to Sean. 'You hide from me. You need to learn how to look after the animals. You're the one who will care for them in the years to come.'

Sean blurted out, 'I don't want to. I hate it!'

Their father raged, shouted, *'Want*? What we want doesn't matter. We don't get what we *want*! We do what we can to survive! What has *want* got to do with the way we live? There is no *want* in the Villas, only need and we'll need someone to care for the animals!'

Sean was crying now. Michael wanted to reach out to him but he didn't dare. His hands and arms were fixed at his side as if he were bound. Care, their father said. There was no care, only maintenance and constriction and fear until death.

'You both need to learn,' their father said. 'You both need to learn what this world really is.' He stopped, went down on one knee, grabbed at the boys' shoulders, pulled them close, dropped his voice to an echoing whisper. His breath smelled of the homebrew, the poison. 'It's not your fault; you don't know what it's like out there. I need to show you so that you can understand why we live like this and so that you can protect yourselves.' He turned to Michael. 'You're good at the game, the best of all the children. You'll be chosen soon to go outside, into the world. You'll need to be more than just fast and silent. You'll need to know what to do when you come across one of those things.'

Michael fought his stammer to ask, 'What things?'

The father turned back to both children. 'I'll show you.' He stood, grabbed an axe, a smaller hatchet, and his bunch of keys from the table. He stuffed the axe handle first into the back of his trousers, pocketed the keys and walked to the back door. 'Come with me.'

The two boys, heads down, blinking back tears, followed out into their yard, into the alley, into the Lansdowns' yard next door. He took his bunch of keys from his pocket, selected one and let them in through the back door.

It was dark in the kitchen, no lights, the late-evening sun leaving just a sliver of blood-red sky visible through the kitchen window.

The boys stayed silent as their father moved to the kitchen door. He gripped the handle and stopped, turned to his sons. 'What you'll see will scare you, but you've got to be brave. You're both strong, both my strong little men. You'll be big men one day. This will help you to grow.' He pushed open the door and beckoned the boys to the open doorway.

It was dark in the room and at first the boys couldn't see anything. As their eyes adjusted they realised that there was little to see; the room was empty, no table or chairs like there was in their own house. Nothing on the walls, no shelves, no pictures. The only break in the monotony was the yawning black hole of the fireplace.

And a smell. That smell. That permanent smell. That smell that Michael only noticed when it disappeared in a gust of wind only to return moments later. It was in the room, filled it, squeezed into every molecule of air, stronger than ever. He gagged, heard Sean do the same.

Their father nudged them inside and as they took their first steps into the room, they became aware of movement behind the open door. Michael stopped, Sean too, neither daring to look. Their father pushed them again, not hard but inescapably. The boys peered around the open door; in the alcove between the chimney breast and the window there was a pile of something, clothes or sheets or...

It moved. The boys heard the rattle of chains. They stepped back into their father, his body hard and unyielding. As the thing rose, they pressed back against him, but he wouldn't move. He held their shoulders, his grip tight and painful, stopping them from trying to move around him.

The thing lurched to its feet, its limbs, torso and head suddenly obvious, its hair, wispy and wild, made a corona by the faint light from the window behind. It stumbled towards them, arms outstretched, head jerking back and forth, mouth opening into a gasping shout of hunger.

Sean screamed, tried to slip out of their father's grip but the father held him firm. Michael was frozen, rooted, helpless as the thing threw itself at them. He squeezed his eyes shut, waited for thing to grab him.

The sound of chains snapping tight. And nothing happened.

He opened his eyes, saw the thing reaching for him, its fingers curling to claws just centimetres from his face. The smell; it smothered him, crawled into his mouth and nose, choked at this throat. He jerked his head back against their father's chest, tried to reach out to Sean and hold his hand, but only managed to grab at the material of his t-shirt. He twisted his hand into a fist, held onto his brother's clothing, held on for dear life.

The thing didn't stop trying to reach them. It pulled uselessly against its chains, reaching and stretching as if it were drowning; desperate, as if it expected them to save it. It grunted, gasped, growled, snarled, shuffled its feet, swung its shoulders and arms and grabbed empty air with its clawed fingers. But the chains held. It couldn't get any closer.

Slowly, their father's grip loosened and became less painful, but his hands remained on their shoulders. 'This is it,' he said, 'this is one of the monsters that fill the outside.'

'It's a person,' Michael said. He could feel their father nodding. 'What's happened to them?'

'They died,' their father said. 'You remember that we teach you never to be alone with a dead body?' The two boys nodded. 'Well, *this* is why.' He paused, his grip loosening further. 'I'm going to turn on a light. You need to be ready. Do not scream. Do you understand? It is important that you do not scream. Being able to look at these things is important, maybe the most important thing. You must look at them if you're to kill them. It's not enough to hit them - they don't feel pain, not like you and me – you must be able to hit them carefully. You must get the brain.'

Michael felt their father's hand lift from his shoulder, drew in a breath and held it.

Light flooded the corner of the room, dazzling back from the window, making both of the boys shut their eyes and raise their hands to shield themselves from the glare.

'Open your eyes,' their father demanded.

Michael blinked, squinted into the glare. The thing still reached at them, still pulled at its chains, still gasped its desperation, still needed them.

'How...?' Michael couldn't find the words to form his question. Slowly, he was able to focus on the thing, its face. It was Mrs Lansdown. Except it wasn't. Even as he pushed back against their father, Michael forced himself to look at this thing. It looked like Mrs Lansdown but that was where all similarities ended. She had been their neighbour, a carer who just wanted to see the two boys smile as they ate her chicken pies and her gravy and her mashed potatoes. This was not her, not her body, her arms, her grasping fingers, her snapping teeth. And her eyes. Empty, yellowed, staring at nothing. This was hunger.

Michael turned away, pushing his cheek into their father's chest, but their father grabbed at his head, turned him to face the thing again. 'Look at it,' he insisted. 'This is what fills the world.'

'Why?' Michael stammered. 'Why are you doing this?'

'You have to be able to kill them,' their father said. 'The brain; it has to be the brain!'

Sean was crying again, sobbing loudly. The father grabbed at him, tried to put his hot, heavy hand over his mouth. 'Hush,' he said. 'You're my little man. You can do anything if you're brave enough.' Sean shook his head over and over, tried to force his mouth away from their father's hand. His face reddened, his eyes widened. Their father's hand was over his nose now. It stank of sweat and animals. 'Be brave!' he shouted. Sean squealed, but the noise was muffled, muted by the huge hand over his face. He struggled on, writhing and kicking. Their father let go of Michael, used two hands to try to subdue his younger son, shouting louder and louder for him to be brave, to be strong, to do as he was told. The thing that was Mrs Lansdown strained at her chains, snarling and gasping. Sean cried and cried, his wails still muffled by their father's hand. The sweat stood out on his bright red face, his eyes bulged, his hands, tiny compared with their father's, grabbed and pulled uselessly at their father's arm, his sweat-wet fingers slipping on the tanned, hairy skin.

In the middle of it all, Michael stood transfixed by the chaos. He watched his little brother's face turn purple, watched their father tighten his grip by wrapping his arm around Sean's torso and squeezing him tight to stop him whipping his body to-and-fro, watched Mrs Lansdown try to reach out to them and then to him, her hands confused, her head jerking back and forth, teeth snapping and grinding. The room spun in a spiral of violence.

Suddenly dizzy, Michael stumbled, staggered into Mrs Lansdown, her fingers curling into his t-shirt, pulling him close, wrenching his face towards her mouth. He jerked his head back just as her teeth would have snapped into his jaw. He felt spittle and drool splash into his face, grunted his disgust and tried to push himself away from her, from it. He lost his balance, falling to the floor, the thing that had been Mrs Lansdown crashing down on top of him, its forehead smashing into his nose, the blood gushing instantly, flooding across his face, into his mouth even as the thing raised its head to lunge again at his face. He raised his hands to push it away, got a hold of its jaw and managed to stop its advance. He tried to shift hands to get a better grip, his sweating palms slipping against its cold flesh, running along its jaw, grabbing at her ears. He pushed against it, tried to lift his legs to force it away, but it was heavy and strong. Its face lowered towards his, jaw moving, teeth snapping, drool dripping, yellowed eyes burning into his. With his left hand, he let go of one ear, grabbed at the jaw, fought for a grip, wrapped his fingers around its teeth, pushed again.

Snap. It clamped its teeth into the knuckles of his fingers, biting through flesh and into bone. The pain hit Michael just as he heard the crunch of his bones. It hit him like a wall of fire, burning his whole body, making him thrash as if he had been set alight. He didn't notice as gouts of his own blood dropped from the thing's mouth and fell into his face, into his mouth, his nose, his eyes. The world turned red as he screamed and screamed in pain. He pushed against its jaw, grabbed at its hair with his other hand and pushed it up, away from his face. It ground its teeth into his fingers, tearing through flesh, crushing bone.

Finally, their father was there, pulling at the thing, grabbing it by the hair and dragging it away. The thing's teeth remained clamped and the last of the skin and flesh that held Michael's fingers tore like hot tar sticking to the heels of shoes on a hot summer's day. The thing was gone, its mouth filled with Michael's fingers, his blood spilling down its chin. The father was screaming his rage, his fear, his shame. He pushed the thing down onto the tiled floor, grabbed at its ears and beat its head into the hard floor. He smashed its skull over and over, screaming at it, his foul words incoherent, his voice blasting the room, filling it, squeezing into every space, every gap, every crack in the wall, and morphing into an apoplectic force of agony.

Michael drew his tattered hand into his breast, tried to grab at the ends of his fingers, tried to stop the bleeding. The pain burned on, made him sick. The room blurred, faded, span around him, their father's angry shouts mixing with a spiralling lightbulb.

Sean's face, tear-streaked, terrified, dumb, hovered over him, his eyes flitting across Michael's face and body in a panicked dance. He was shouting, but Michael couldn't hear him.

Then their father was above him, sweating and terrified, the axe in his hand. He was pulling Michael's left arm away from his breast, trying to straighten it on the floor. Michael protested, tried to pull his arm back but their father gripped him too tightly, holding his wrist to the floor. Their father was shaking his head, speaking to him, saying the same word over and over. Michael couldn't hear him but he could see that he was saying sorry.

The axe was above his head. Their father hesitated, looked right into his eyes, said sorry again before turning away, suddenly unable to meet his eyes and focusing on his arm.

Michael struggled against the spinning room, against the pain, against their father's weight as it held him down. But he couldn't move.

The axe dropped. Michael felt it smash into his skin, into his bone, felt the pain, the wall of fire curling around him and forming a well into which he'd been thrown. He fell into the darkness and burned to oblivion.

The boys' bedroom was at the back of 11 Victoria Villas. To the boys it was the front; the grown-ups called it the back because of how they remembered the world: the street was the front and the yards and the alley were the back. But to the boys, the yards and the alley were the whole world: their work, their play, their education. They went into the houses to sleep and to clean and to eat. They were animals, the houses were their pens, the yards and alley their limited freedoms.

For the grown-ups the 'front' was a world lost to angels and monsters. To the children, this 'front' was an unknown stage covered with boards, the setting fading and covered with dust, the spotlights dim, the actors waiting lifetimes for their cues.

Years ago, Michael had learned in class that Victoria Villas was just the name for the row of houses on their side and that the street outside, at the 'front', was Jubilee Street. He hadn't understood. The teacher had shown him pictures of streets. She called them terraced streets. Two rows of front doors and windows separated by a road. She said that the pictures weren't of Jubilee Street but they were very similar. And then she'd said that only the houses on Michael's side were called Victoria Villas, that the other side was Albert Villas and they were on a street called Edward Street and that Edward was the son of Victoria and Albert and that he'd become king and that he'd been the seventh Edward but he'd been a womaniser and had had a string of affairs with actresses but he was king but only for nine years and then there'd been a George, Edward's eldest son, and he was the fifth George and he was king during World War One and...

Michael's head had spun. There was – there had been - a wide world of royalty and empire and class and industry and agriculture and cities and poverty and countries and continents and war and literature and sport and film and wonders and injustices and liberties and constrictions.

She'd gone on to talk about the size of London and the millions of people who had lived there – lived here. She said that if they were able to stand on the roofs they would see a city, miles of streets just like the ones in the pictures and churches and huge buildings, as big and bigger than the warehouse at the end of the Villas, and in the distance skyscrapers and towers. She'd told them about the Houses of Parliament and how Victoria Villas was just close enough to hear Big Ben strike the hour every hour. Michael remembered London, the noise and the bustle of the crowds and traffic. Cars and vans, mostly electric and quiet but the occasional older vehicle that excited their father as it roared through the streets. And the buses, huge and red and so loud. That was smell from the past. Petrol and diesel engines. That was before Sean was born. Michael had always felt special that he had memories of things from before the Message. Little things, smells and noises and the feel of the poles on a bus as the engine rumbled away from the stop. He kept them like treasures, like the memories of his mum. His own extracts from his own DVD.

He stared at his bedroom ceiling, trying to manage the pain. It lived within him now, an unwelcome, raucous guest. Their father had told him that he would have to find ways of living with it. Cohabiting, he'd said. Michael had never heard the word before, but he thought back to his lessons and remembered words like habitat and habitation and cooperate and cooperation, and he thought he knew what their father meant.

It was hard. He couldn't focus on anything else. He couldn't read, couldn't watch DVDs, couldn't talk with Sean or with the other children who'd been allowed to visit. That pain distracted him, bothered him, tugged and nagged at him, chewing on his arm, sometimes creeping up into his shoulder and chest, other times racing through his whole body, charging round and round like a whirlwind of fire blowing through him, like his body was the Villas, just yards and an alley and every part burned in a conflagration that would swallow their whole world.

Only their father distracted him. His face, the guilt, the shame, it was etched there, carved into his features. He smelled worse all the time. He wasn't washing, was drinking more of the homebrew. He came to Michael, sat at his bedside, held his hand, soothed the pain or at least allowed Michael to focus on something else. It was like the pain itself wanted to study this thing, this man, this once-father-turned-maimer. It settled within Michael and watched, timed the tears – they always came – and listened as he spoke of the pigs' and chickens' health, the way Sean couldn't, or wouldn't, keep the sties and run as clean as Michael always had. How Michael had always been such a good boy, such a good little man and how he was going to have be a better man than their father had ever been and how he would need to be strong and brave to live with the pain and how he knew that his best boy would be able to do it. Easily, he sometimes said. With help, he sometimes said. All alone, he sometimes said.

Michael watched him too. Tried to recognise him. Tried to understand. Tried to force his stammer back into his voice when their father was with him, but it was gone. He spoke smoothly, with no delay to their father. Michael tried not to hate their father.

That lived with him too. That was another cohabitation. Hate and pain. The former the only thing that cooled the latter.

Sometimes, he would clench his fists. He would swear that he could feel both fists clenching as he listened to their father begin to cry and the apologies begin again, muffled behind the hands that he used to cover his face, slurred by the homebrew.

His bandaged wrist still spotted with blood two weeks after that night. The dots would form while he slept, providing an excruciating alarm call at 5am each day. It was just another number on the clock; Michael slept fitfully, the pain never allowing him more than an hour or two of sleep. He'd seen all of the numbers on that clock in the last two weeks.

Sean would go days without coming to see him. Michael pictured him in the warehouse, flopped belly first on a roll of carpet, both hands stretched around it, his cheek resting against the soft surface. He watched him slide from the roll and drift to the shutter, place both of his hands against the metal and lean his cheek against the cool, hard surface. Sean listened, whispered, smiled, cried. He drifted back to the control box, lingered at the keyhole, wished...

Michael had been alone for hours, had dozed, struggled to live with the pain, ached for distraction and dreaded visitors. He was ashamed, he realised, ashamed of his sudden deformity. He lifted his arm into view; the white bandage tapered to an end just above where his wrist had been. Their father said over and over that he had been lucky, that he had taken the hand quickly and so no more of his arm would be amputated. It had been a good outcome from a bad situation; it could have been so much worse. Their father said that a lot. So much worse. Michael stared at the bandage, wondered at how thin it was at the end. So much worse.

The quiet was broken as Sean burst into the room, shouting Michael's name. 'What? What is it?' Michael asked, his heart racing with the shock.

'It's Big Ben! It's ringing!'

'The clock?'

The bell! It's ringing. It started yesterday. You have to listen hard to hear it, but once you know it's there you can't hear anything else.' Sean raced to the window and threw it open. 'Listen!'

Michael listened, couldn't hear anything and shook his head.

'Concentrate!' Sean demanded. 'Really listen. It's Big Ben! Mr Ellis says so. He says he used to listen to it every day and he swears it's Big Ben. There are people in the world, Mike, not just monsters! You've got to hear it! Listen. Really listen!'

'What does that mean, 'really listen'?'

'Like in the game when you're waiting to grab. You know how to do it. Listen as hard as you can.'

Michael listened. He did his best to ignore Sean's excited breathing and the thumping of his own heart, the pulsing pain of his arm. The two boys waited a full minute before Sean let out an exasperated groan.

'Come to the window!' Sean demanded.

Michael shook his head. He hadn't left his bed since that night. Their father had helped him with a bed pan, washed him, changed his sheets. Michael had let him do it all. Let him busy himself, make himself feel better. Let him see his own son's weaknesses and wounds, day after day. Let him see what he had done. It was only their father who ever saw his shortened arm, the bloody bandage; he wouldn't let anyone else see it. Michael stayed in bed not just to rest and to heal but to punish their father.

'Come on!'

'No, I can't.'

'You can.' Sean ran at the bed, ripped the quilt away. He saw his brother's arm, the bandage, the red spots, paused for just half a second, but it was long enough for Michael.

'Get out!' he shouted. 'Get out!'

Sean staggered back from the bed. 'I'm sorry,' he said. 'It's not my fault - you never show it! That's the first time I've seen it, what do you expect me to do?'

'Just go!' Michael was grabbing at his quilt with both hands, the left waving uselessly in the air in front of it. 'Just go!' he shouted again. He grabbed at the quilt but couldn't pull it up onto the bed. It was just a quilt. How could he be so weak? He cried in frustration, real tears spilling down his cheeks. 'Just go,' he said, his stammer back again, fighting with the pain and his quivering lower lip and his gasping sobs.

Sean didn't leave. He moved to his brother, helped to pull the quilt back up on to the bed, covering his arm, and sitting next to him, reaching awkwardly for his brother's shoulders, pulling him close and letting him sob onto his own shoulder, soaking his t-shirt.

Michael clung to Sean with one arm, grabbing at his brother with his one hand and twisting his fist into the material of his t-shirt.

They stayed like that for a long time, until Sean said, 'Come on. Come listen.'

Michael allowed himself to be helped to the edge of the bed. Sean was too small to do much more than help him to balance, but he managed to get to his feet, slowly, warily, and shuffle over to the open window. He liked the air on his face, cool on his tear-soaked cheeks, felt, suddenly, the weeks of confinement in his room.

'Listen,' Sean insisted.

Michael stood at the window, squinting into the brightness, frowning as he concentrated. Sean looked up at him, expectantly, eagerly.

There. And again.

On the third, Michael looked down at his brother and smiled. 'Big Ben,' he said. Sean nodded, shared his smile, made it wider.

A thump on the window. Another.

'What's that?' Sean asked.

Michael stared at the fly as it bounced against the window again. It was fat and black. 'A fly,' he said.

'What's a fly?'

Michael stared at his little brother, confused by the question until he remembered that there had been no flies. The grown-ups had talked about it a lot in the first and second summers. Where were all the flies? In the first summer they used the end of the year-long night to explain it but in the second they were confused. By the third it was barely mentioned. This was a world without flies. Might have fewer spiders, Mrs Lansdown had said. She'd smiled at her husband who had smiled back at her. Michael closed his eyes, willed the memory of the Lansdowns away. 'It's an insect that flies. I guess that's why they're called flies. They used to be pretty common.'

Sean leaned at the windowpane. 'It's ugly,' he said. It landed on the window, crawled across the glass, paused, rubbed its front legs. Sean grimaced at it. 'Disgusting.' He looked closer. 'It's like a mini monster.' Michael leaned close. It was disgusting. He couldn't remember flies looking like this thing. It looked evil. Sean reached out and closed the window then tapped at the glass. The fly launched away.

'Open the window,' said Michael. 'I want to listen.'

Sean smiled as he opened the window. 'There's going to be a *mission*,' he said. He relished the word. 'The grown-ups are going to go and see why it's ringing. I bet they would've taken you before...' His voice trailed away. Both boys looked down at his arm. 'Sorry,' Sean whispered.

'It's fine. Don't worry.' Michael shuffled back to his bed. Sean was right; now that he had heard it he couldn't help but listen to it. It pulsed through him, racing along his veins with the pain, as if the bell and his pain twisted together to run and play, each tempering the other. He slumped into his bed, exhausted by his tiny trip. 'Don't think I'd be much use on a mission right now.'

Sean came to join his brother. His eyes lost their focus as he spoke. 'Imagine it, Mike,' he said. 'I bet there's a whole new world out there.'

'A brave new world,' Michael said.

Sean nodded, laughing. He'd been Miranda in a production of 'The Tempest' the children had performed last Christmas. Ms Scott had helped them to put it on. They'd changed the language into normal English – she had rolled her eyes at the children's insistence that no one would understand if they didn't, but she had helped them to re-write it. That was everyone's Christmas wish, a brave new world. Michael had desperately wanted to be Prospero, but he'd allowed another boy to bully Ms Scott into letting him have it. Sean had badgered at his brother at the time, telling him over and over that he would be the best boy for the part. The grown-ups had laughed, drunk homebrew, laughed some more and then cried. Mrs Lansdown assured all the children they were tears of joy, but none of them were fooled; they cried for the people in the world that they'd lost and for the world that never was, the world promised by the Message.

'It must be a new message, that's what Mr Ellis is saying,' said Sean.

'What does Dad say?' Michael asked.

Sean's face darkened. 'Not much,' he said. 'He keeps to himself. None of the other grown-ups speak to him. Not much, anyway. I think they know what he did. I think that he had Mr Lansdown waiting for us too. I think he wanted us each to kill a monster.' Sean was talking fast, letting the words he'd been keeping back for two weeks tumble out. 'He was talking about it on the night. He was saying that he only wanted for us to be stronger, that he was only doing what a father should do, making boys into men. He was talking about it like we were soldiers or something, like we needed to be able to fight better. He said that he needed to take care of Mr

Lansdown. He kept talking about Mr Lansdown while he was dealing with your arm. He was stitching your skin back together – it was gross! - and talking about Mr Lansdown and worrying about someone else finding him. He kept correcting himself and calling Mr Lansdown 'it' instead. I didn't know what he meant but when he'd finished bandaging your arm and he left me here I realised that he must mean that Mr Lansdown was just like Mrs Lansdown.' Sean stopped, grimaced an apology at his brother for bringing back terrible memories, then plunged on. 'He'd kept looking at me when he was talking about Mr Lansdown. Kept talking about being able to work on animals and how I'd just needed to be a little braver and how Mr Lansdown was supposed to help me to be braver.'

Sean stopped again. 'It was my fault, Mike! Dad said over and over how I needed to be braver, how it should've been me taking care of Mr Lansdown while you dealt with Mrs Lansdown. If I hadn't cried so much you wouldn't have been bitten, that's what he meant.'

Michael was shaking his head, reaching out to his brother, trying to soothe at his shoulder. 'It's okay, it's not your fault,' he said. He said it over and over again, but Sean wasn't listening; he needed to talk.

'If I'd done what Dad wanted. If I'd been stronger, braver, we would have dealt with it. The brain, that's all I had to do, get it in the brain. That's what he must've gone to do when he left me alone. That's why we were alone, Mike, because I couldn't do what needed to be done!'

Slowly, Sean's confessions were lost in his tears, his gasping sobs. He clung to Michael. 'I'm sorry. I'm sorry. I'm sorry...'

Michael could only think about their father. Sean's cries became distant, still loud, but separate, like they were in another room. Michael's pain shared that room, along with sorrow and despair. Here, now, in this room, on this bed, in this embrace, there was just one thing. Hate. He hated their father. He would hide it no more. 'It's okay,' he said to Sean. 'It's okay.'

Six grown-ups, Mr Ellis, Ms Scott, Mr Murray and three of the outsiders, younger residents of the Villas who went outside regularly, left the next day. Michael told Sean to try to get a look as they exited at the 'front'. He realised that he was worried about Ms Scott. He didn't care about Mr Ellis and his homebrew. Mr Murray was one of the plumbers. Michael didn't know him well. He'd heard other grown-ups make jokes about sweets called Murray mints. He couldn't remember ever trying such a thing before the crash.

He wished their father was going. He was glad he was staying. He didn't want him to come to his room. He waited impatient hours between visits.

'Did you see the outside?' Michael asked Sean later.

Sean shook his head. 'We couldn't get near. All the grown-ups met in number one. They were in there for ages.'

'Probably doing last checks and stuff.' There were always parties that left the Villas, looking for supplies and keeping an eye on the surrounding area. They always set out from number one as this was only door that wasn't barred against the outside world. Their father had talked briefly about other survivors and how they couldn't be trusted. Mr Wilson shared the house with Mr Rodriguez. They were both American, both big and strong. Michael liked them; they were jolly and confident, especially Mr Rodriguez. They were in charge of the foraging and scouting missions as well as the other outsiders who lived at number one. Michael had lost track of how many there were, maybe five, six or seven of them. Mostly, they kept to themselves. But, Michael considered, even though they were used to going outside, this mission was bigger, more important than any before, so they must have taken their time making sure everything was okay. The outsiders were good at what they did and always careful, and the grown-ups, especially Mr Wilson and Mr Rodriguez, would make sure they stayed that way. Michael remembered their father's words about him being good at the game and how he would soon be selected to go outside. He looked down at his bandages. They were still white; their father had changed them that morning. Michael had tried to ask him about the mission, but he'd been reluctant to talk about it.

'Dad thinks it's too dangerous,' said Sean. He too was staring at the clean bandages. Michael no longer kept his arm hidden under the quilt. The pain was still constant but less, more manageable. It seemed to enjoy being in the sight of others, like it was proud somehow. Sean switched his eyes from the bandaged stump and back to his brother. 'He thinks anyone who wants to draw that much attention to themselves must setting some kind of trap.'

'Why would anyone do that?'

Sean shrugged. 'He thinks that no one would be stupid enough to make so much noise unless they thought they could gain something from it.'

'The angels!' Michael exclaimed.

'That's what Dad said, too. He said that the bell would bring angels and how could anyone deal with lots of angels all at once?'

'Or just one,' said Michael. Sean nodded. 'Did any of the grown-ups agree with him?'

Sean shrugged again. 'Dad was telling me about it; I haven't heard what the other grown-ups have said.'

'There can't have been many if the mission is still going ahead.'

The boys stared out of the bedroom window; the blue sky apparently endless beyond the rooftops of the Villas.

'Maybe it's an all-clear,' said Michael. 'Like the birdsong.'

'That's a warning.'

'*And* an all clear. Maybe someone's found a way to stop it all and they're telling us it's okay. Maybe there are hundreds of people out there who can hear the bell and they'll come to it and join together. Someone could be trying to get London back like it was.'

Sean was excited by Michael's words, his face bright and shining. 'More grown-ups,' he said. 'We need more grown-ups.' The boys had seen what happened to the adults who lived in the Villas; sometimes they stalked and stomped around the Villas like giants locked in cages, at other times they just sat and stared, like the bars of their cages were too close to let them move. So many of them had given up. What does *want* have to do with anything, their father had said. Adults didn't want anything beyond butter, extra eggs and homebrew.

'It's not fair,' Sean continued. 'Dad can't be it; he can't be all we have.' The boys imagined the Villas without the Lansdowns and Ms Scott and they saw their father alone in the alley, his bag of medicines and knives at his side, his face pale; Death living with them here at the Villas.

Michael spoke. 'If they all get together, all of the grown-ups in the world, they can sort everything out. We could live in the world, not in the Villas.'

Sean was nodding. 'We could get out through the warehouse,' he said.

That broke the spell for Michael. Sean had left something unsaid: he wanted their mother to help them. 'It's not Mum,' said Michael. 'It can't be.'

Tears shone in Sean's eyes as he nodded. 'I know,' he said.

'Even if it was Mum, she would be like Mrs Lansdown.'

Sean nodded again. 'I know.'

Michael studied his brother and was either satisfied or the pain in his arm meant that he couldn't focus for long. He cradled his shortened arm, the bandaged snout sticking from his loose fingers like the nose of a poorly but still curious pet.

Later in the week, in the afternoon, after Sean had finished his chores, the two brothers were together again. They played cards. Michael was frustrated at how hard it was to deal with his hand with only one hand. He'd said as much, and Sean, unable to stop himself, had laughed, then fallen silent, muttering apologies. Just for second, Michael had been shocked, then he had laughed as well, realising that his pain had receded throughout the day, settled into the background, still pulsing and aching, but gently, almost kindly, as if the pain, his cohabitor, was now also the memory of his missing hand, still remembered, still with him.

'A lot of people are poorly,' said Sean.

'How many?'

Sean shrugged. He laid a card on the quilt, tutted as it slipped off the pile into the folds of the bedding. 'There was no game today because there were only three of us kids. I didn't see a grown-up all day. Dad's been going to them. He's moaning about it. You know how he gets when he has to see to people as well as animals.' Their father was an impatient man at the best of times but when he had to tend to sick people he would complain vociferously when he returned. Animals didn't complain like people, he'd say. If I'd wanted to be a nurse, I wouldn't have bothered with all those years of veterinary school, he'd say. The boys laughed again at the memories of their father's ridiculous rage, then fell quiet as different memories smothered their laughter.

'He said they'd been bitten by the flies,' Sean continued. 'He said he'd never seen anything like it.'

'Flies are gross, but I don't remember them biting.' Michael laid his cards face down, selected one by plucking at the corner, placed it onto the pile, then scooped up his cards again and tried to rearrange them into a fan.

Sean sighed. 'It's a slow game when you do that. Just tell me what card you want to put down and I'll pick it out.'

'I want to do it myself,' Michael said, not too defensively.

Sean frowned his cynicism. 'Anyway, that's what Dad said, the flies-not-biting part.'

'What are they going to do about them?'

Sean shrugged again as he laid another card. 'They've gone.'

'Who've gone?' Michael started the laborious process of laying a card. Sean rolled his eyes.

'Not who, them, the flies. No one's seen one all day and some say they didn't see any yesterday, either. Dad's told people to see if they can see any dead ones and tell him if they do. I've seen some dead ones. They're too gross to go anywhere near, so I just told Dad. He says he's going to try and have a look and see if there's anything weird about them.'

'They sound very weird.'

They played on in silence, Sean tutting and sighing at how slowly Michael played, the two of them laughing together, enjoying their game and their company.

It was dark when Sean woke Michael. The younger brother was whispering, hissing to wake the older. 'Michael! Michael! Wake up!'

The pain flared, angry at being woken. It surged through Michael's arm and into his body, battering at his shoulder and head as it went. He eyes snapped open wide yet blurred.

'Dad says you've got to get up.'

Michael tried to shift the pain, to push it back so that he could sit up, but it was too strong. Sweat broke out across his whole body, then froze, sealing him into his own skin, trapping him with his pain.

Not noticing his brother's struggles, Sean didn't stop speaking. 'Something's wrong. He's scared but not angry. I've never seen him like it before. He says we're not safe. He's saying the Villas aren't safe. That we need to leave. That we can't be here.' Something in Sean's voice, more than just fear or panic, a desperation, a despair, fought its way past Michael's pain, helped him to push it back. 'I think that some of the people, kids and grown-ups, in the Villas have turned like Mrs Lansdown. Dad thinks it was the flies. He thinks it was the bites that have infected them or something. He says that they're dead but they're still going to come for us, just like Mrs Lansdown.'

Michael was up on one elbow, gasping and dizzy. He wanted to be sick but he swallowed the bile back, forced it down into his belly, smothered his pain with it. 'Help me up.' Sean dragged at his brother, pulling ineffectually. Michael shook him off. 'Just give me a minute.'

'We don't have a minute!'

Michael struggled to pull a sling over his head, settle his arm into it.

Then, their father was at the door, rushing in and scooping Michael into his arms. He was quick, unthinking about Michael's pain, unhearing as his son howled. He didn't look down into Michael's face; stared ahead, his eyes fixed on the door, his jaw set against his son's suffering.

They thumped out of the bedroom and along the landing, to the top of the stairs, Michael groaning all the way as he tried to pull his arm further into the sling, closer to his chest, and hold it safe against the doorframes and the walls as their father hurried, Sean at his heels, trying to move purposefully, trying to not to show how scared he was.

Michael was placed on his feet and leaned against the wall. He could feel the wallpaper through the sleeve of his thin t-shirt. He caught a glimpse of the rucksacks piled in the doorway of their father's bedroom, all of them fat and heavy. Their father was bending down in front of him, holding his upper arms and talking into his face. 'You need to be able to move on your own, Mike,' he said. 'We need to go and I need to carry the bags, Sean too, so you need to be able to move. Can you do that?'

Michael stared at their father, the words not making sense, the smell of the homebrew powerful and foul. He shook his head...

'You have to!' their father insisted.

The pain had pushed its way to the front of his mind, wasn't letting him listen, was spitting at their father, taunting him, daring him to shout, to order his son to stand. Michael felt like he was caught between two bullies, each of them insisting he do something that the other would punish him for. Their father gripped his upper arms, started to shake him.

Sean was at their father's shoulder, trying to pull him away. He was shouting. Michael could see his mouth moving, but he couldn't hear; the pain wouldn't let him, forced him to ignore his brother and concentrate on their father; his face was contorted with emotion. Was he angry or scared? Michael shrank back from him, trying to retreat into the pattern of the wallpaper. The pain flared in triumph as their father shook him again.

'Dad! Leave him alone!' Sean's voice cut through the pain. 'Dad!'

Their father shrugged Sean away but the boy was instantly back, two little hands on their father's right shoulder, pulling at him and shouting, his voice screeching through the narrow landing. Their father shoved at him again, harder this time, pushing him down, sending him thudding to his bottom.

'Wait!' Michael called out before Sean could get back to his feet again. 'I can move. It's okay.'

Their father turned to Michael. 'That's my good boy. You're my strong little man, right?' Michael nodded. The father held his shoulders again, squeezed them tight. It hurt but Michael didn't complain, was glad, even, of the distraction of other pain. 'The hardest part is first,' their father said. 'We need to get into the roof space; get over to number one and we can get out of the Villas and go meet up with the team. Maybe we can come back, clear the houses; not waste everything that we've created here. You can do it, Michael. Just one ladder.' Michael nodded again. The father grabbed at a hooked pole and started to unscrew the roof space hatch. Michael looked around their father, caught

Sean's eye, tried to nod his adequacy to him. Sean tried to smile back. The roof space hatch dropped and their father unfolded the ladder, the abrasive noise of the aluminium loud and piercing.

The father was loading a rucksack onto Sean's back and tightening the straps. It was huge, over his head and down to his thighs. He staggered, almost stumbling back and had to grab the ladder to keep himself upright. 'Go!' their father hissed.

Sean started up the ladder, heaving his combined weight one slow step at a time. Halfway, the rucksack wedged in the gap. 'I can't move!' he called down.

'Push harder,' their father whispered.

'I'm pushing as hard as I can!'

'Keep your voice down. You must be silent up there.' He stepped onto the bottom rung of the ladder and started to push at Sean.

Michael could see that it was useless. 'Dad,' he said. He slapped at his back. 'Dad!' Their father turned, looking down on his eldest. 'You'll have to put the bag up separately.' Their father's face twisted as the internal conflict played out in his features. Something seemed to give and he stepped down, nodding.

'You're right,' he whispered. He leaned down, close to Michael's face. 'I'm rushing.' He tried to smile. 'I'm panicking. Your dad's got a panic on!' he said and tried to turn the smile into a laugh, causing a fresh blast of the stench of homebrew. He turned back to Sean. 'Come down. Let's do this right.'

Minutes later, their father, visibly calmer, had pushed three fat rucksacks into the roof space and Sean was climbing the ladder. Every step was a loud metallic creak, like a wheezing, broken accordion.

Michael was next. He grasped the side of the ladder with his hand.

'No,' their father whispered. 'You'll be better holding the rung, not the side; you'll have better balance that way.'

Michael nodded, grabbed at the rung a step above his head, took a deep breath as he tried to anticipate how his pain would react and pulled himself one step up. His pain lifted its lion's head, looked all through Michael, tensed, readied itself.

'That's great,' their father whispered. His head was still taller than Michael and he bobbed his head to speak into his ear.

Sean smiled down from the roof space, his head small, so far away. 'Come on, Mike!' he called down.

Michael nodded, leant against the ladder to balance while he reached up to the next rung. He paused, took another deep breath. Climbed another rung. His pain circled him, waiting.

'You're doing great,' their father whispered again, their heads level now. Michael caught another draught of his breath. Sean's face, eager, scared, so far above.

A third step. A fourth. Michael's head started to spin as his breathing grew louder, the sweat on his palm thicker, his pulse stronger. His pain stepped into his pulse, its great paws splashing as it waded into his blood.

'Keep going. I've got you.'

Halfway. Taller than their dad now, and exhausted. As he pulled at the next rung, his sweat-slicked palm slipped. Their father caught him. 'I've got you,' he said. Michael's arm was crushed against the rungs of the ladder. Pain saw its chance, leapt at him, at his blood. It ran through him, roaring his agony. He called out in pain, clutched at the ladder with his hand, pressed against it with his thighs, tried to free his arm, tried not to cry, tried not to burn as the pain tore through him. Tears slashed at his hot cheeks, fell unobstructed onto their father's face.

'It's okay. You're okay. You're doing great. Just keep going. I've got you.'

Michael shook his head. 'I can't.'

'You can.'

Michael looked up, away from their father and into Sean's face not so far above him. Nearly there. Sean was close enough to reach down and soothe and clutch at his shoulder. 'You're so close, Mike,' he said.

Michael let their father hold him, lifted his hand to the next rung, fought back the pain. Grabbed, squeezed tight, hauled himself up, their father pushing, Sean instinctively pulling at his shirt.

'Just let me help, Sean,' said their father. 'You'll upset his balance.' Sean withdrew, his head disappearing, then reappearing, a frown etched into his brow.

With their father's support, Michael climbed another step and another, his head emerging into the dark roof space, then his shoulders. Sean scuffled back across the dusty boards. 'That's it,' he whispered. 'You're doing it.'

Michael had his elbow on the floor. 'Help me,' he said to his brother. Sean dashed forward, grabbed at Michael's hand, flinched at how hot he was, but held him tightly. Michael inched up the ladder, still supported by their father and leaning against Sean as he was finally able to sit on the lip of the hatch. He flopped back, raised his legs to roll away from the hole, head dizzy, heart hammering, breath ragged, pain out of control, blurring his vision, making him want to be sick. He rolled onto his side, vomited just as their father climbed into the roof space.

He was down on his knees in an instant, feeling at Michael's forehead, scooping his other hand behind his shoulders and raising him into a sitting position. Michael gasped and sobbed, his head lolling across his chest, his mouth slack, drool adding to the sweat that already made his shirt cling to his skinny frame.

'You're burning up,' said their father. He looked around the space as if he thought that someone would come forward and help him. He smoothed Michael's sweat-soaked hair away from his face. 'I'm sorry, Michael,' he said. 'We've got to keep moving. Sean, come help your brother.' Their father stood and stepped away from Michael, let Sean move close and arranged Michael's head onto his little brother's knee. 'Rest for a few minutes.'

He moved to the rucksacks, came back with water, holding a bottle to Michael's lips. Michael grabbed at it, thirsty, squeezing the plastic, guzzled at the water that shot forth, gulping, splashing.

Michael felt the water flood and cool his body. It felt good, the pain was forced to recede a little, and as he rested, his heart slowing, his pulse calming, his pain skulked back to its repose, settled again, but kept its head in the air, watching, waiting.

Their father had strapped a rucksack to his chest and back, giving him a huge silhouette. Sean shrugged into his pack, a tiny turtle with an over-sized shell. The two went to Michael to help him to his feet but Michael waved them away. He rolled onto his knees, his palm flat against the boarding. He pushed himself up onto one foot and then two. His pain reared again, but Michael remembered the time they had already spent together, the long weeks in his room when they had learned to live together. He wiped at his face, smearing the tear-streaked dust, and in his mind he held out the ghost of his left hand and took the paw of his pain. It gripped him, claws sinking into his flesh. Michael saw this thing for what it was: his life. He was alive because of this pain. Here, in the darkness and the dust of the roof space, he could see it clearly. He looked up at their father, saw the desperate guilt, saw the overarching desire to keep them safe, to let them live in this world of angels and monsters, saw it and let his hate recede along with his pain. In that moment, he could begin to understand, could begin to forgive him. He smiled, their father frowning with concern, and held out his right hand to let their father pull him slowly, painfully, to his feet.

'Let's go,' said Michael.

The three of them, father and two sons, set off towards number one, picking their way between the demolished walls that had separated the properties' loft spaces. They needed to pass over six houses till number one, the first house of the row but the last on their journey.

'What happened?' Michael asked.

'The fly bites,' said Sean. 'First, they were ill, then they died.'

'And the dead do not stay still,' said their father.

Their whispers echoed from the underside of the roof tiles. Here and there they could see chinks of fading evening light as the last rays of the sun sought to share their shelter.

'Like Mrs Lansdown,' said Michael.

'And Mr Lansdown,' Sean added. He didn't try to hide the bitterness in his voice.

Their father nodded, pursed his lips, stared ahead. He had a hatchet in each of the side strappings of his front rucksack. As they neared the last house, he took hold of one, gripping it firmly.

'We lost track of who had been bitten,' their father said. 'I lost track,' he corrected. 'By midday yesterday, I was the only one left.'

'No other kids either,' said Sean.

'No one answers their door when I knock,' their father continued. 'But I can see movement. The houses are full of deads.'

'Deads?' Michael asked.

'It's what we call them,' said their father. He stowed the hatchet and took a torch from the front pocket of the front rucksack, his arms reaching around to grope with zips and clips. Light flooded the space. Michael hadn't realised how dark it was. Their father handed the torch to Michael and took up the hatchet again. Michael lit the way to the final hatch and the three of them stood around it, staring at the pile of folded ladders that shined silver in the torchlight.

'That leads to the landing,' their father said. 'The house won't be empty; Wilson and Rodriguez will be in there as well as the rest of the outsiders. No one was answering the door two hours ago.'

'Why didn't you just go in?' Michael asked. Back doors were never locked in the Villas.

'I didn't know what I would find.' He gripped the hatchet. 'This way, I can be fairly sure we can get in without any trouble.'

'Why?' Sean asked.

Their father looked down at his youngest son, his face shadowed by the light from the torch. 'Deads don't climb stairs and it's hard to imagine anyone dying suddenly on a landing.' He shrugged off his rucksacks, grabbed at a pole provided for just this circumstance and opened the hatch, letting it fall into the space below and pushing the ladder with the pole to unfold it. Metallic squeaks and creaks screamed through the roof space and, they had to assume, the house below.

They stared down into the landing below, the ladders stretching straight to the bare wooden floorboards, its feet caught in the pool of light from Michael's torch, looking like the metal feet of a moon lander.

'I'll go first,' their father said. 'You can lower the bags to me.' He placed his big boot on the top step, trying to move slowly, but they had made so much noise already that Michael wondered at the effort. Halfway, their father paused, listened. Satisfied that he was alone in the narrow space, he trousered the hatchet and held up his hand to take the torch from Michael, then descended to the floor. He scanned each way with the torch, then turned it up to the boys, dazzling them. They both ducked their heads back. 'I need to check the bedrooms,' he called up.

'Why?' Michael asked. 'Can't we just leave them in there?'

'I will, but I want to know where they all are before we go downstairs.'

The boys waited in the dark and listened to their father's footsteps on the floorboards. They stood close together, shoulder to shoulder. They started at the sound of a bedroom door opening. There was no extra light. Long seconds passed and seemed to stretch into minutes. Neither boy moved, neither dared to breathe.

The torch's beam flooded the landing again and the door closed. The boys gasped their relief. Their father's footsteps came back towards, them, the torch passing beneath carried by a shadow that was their father. Darkness again. Another door, more long seconds, the door closed, the landing lit again, more footsteps, the light receding, another door opened, another wait stretching into the darkness. This time, Michael thought. There will be a scuffle, the torch will drop to the floor, roll onto the landing, show them emptiness, and their father would not return. He turned to Sean, the shape of his head just discernible. Sean was already looking up at him. How would they cope alone? Sean shook his head. What did that mean? Their father was a difficult man to love but without him what would they do? Michael knew; they would feed the pigs and chickens, clean their sties and runs. They would live alone in Victoria Villas, hiding from angels, trying not to smell the smell and living in fear of the other houses and the monsters within.

The light swung back beneath them, and their father's footsteps approached. He didn't pause at the bottom of the steps, instead climbing straight up to the boys, sitting on the boards and indicating that they should sit with him. He placed the torch on its end between them so that it pointed up into the underside of the roof slates, dust floating in its beam.

Their father, his face monochrome in the upturned shadows, spoke. 'All of the rooms upstairs are empty, so there must be at least four of them downstairs. We need to get to the front of the house to get outside.' He stopped, looked at the boys in turn. His face was different, all the anger and impatience were gone, replaced by guilt and regret. He couldn't look into their eyes, Michael noticed. 'So, I've changed my mind; it's too dangerous; we have no idea where they will be when we go downstairs. They could grab us before we even see them.'

'How fast are they?' Michael asked.

'Not fast at all if you can see them.' The two boys were surprised. Sean started to suggest that they could do it, do it easily. Their father stopped him. 'It's like your game; they only move and they only try to grab when they see you. But in your game, how often does anyone make it to the end?'

The boys looked at each other; their father was right. Most days there was no outright winner, just someone who scored highest, maybe four or five or six, depending on the number of players. Nearly every time they were grabbed.

'And it's too dark, but even if we wait for daylight, the front of the house will be pitch black, and that's where our exit is. We're stuck.'

Michael felt his heart rate rise, felt his pain surge, felt the sweat break out anew on his forehead. He cradled his bandaged stump, took the weight off it, let it rest in his palm. He felt like talking to it, to tell it everything was going to be okay.

'We have supplies to wait it out,' their father said. 'The others will be back from the mission and they can clear the house.'

'But they'll be walking into the dark, too,' said Michael. 'They'll be grabbed as soon as they're inside.' Sean nodded his agreement.

Their father shook his head. 'No, we've got a warning system in place. They wait for an answer at the door before they enter – a secret knock, if you like. If they don't get that, they'll know to come in prepared.' He reached out to the boys, gripped their shoulders. 'It's the only way to keep you safe.'

The boys had been told about their safety their whole lives in the Villas, about how their father only wanted them to be safe. He'd made sure time and again that they understood his need for their safety. He'd hammered that message home along with his frustration and impatience. This was the longest they had spent together without him threatening something or promising some consequence of their stupidity. But now it was him that considered the consequences, and they were dire.

Their father shook his head. 'We can wait for days, a whole week in necessary. We'll be okay.'

'The warehouse!' Sean exclaimed. Michael and their father stared at him, both too shocked to remind him to be quiet. 'We can go out through the warehouse,' said Sean, whispering again.

Their father glowered at him, remembering the boys' disobedience. They cowered, wilting in his glare as they waited for him to upbraid them. Instead, he said, 'That area is secured.'

Relieved, Sean nodded. 'I know, but we can get out through the shutter. There's another room on the other side, right? We get into it through the shutter and then outside from there.'

Their father leaned back a little to give himself time to think. 'It's a shop,' he said, 'a carpet shop, but no one has been through that shutter for years,' he said. 'We've got no idea what's on the other side.'

Michael watched Sean as he responded, looking for signs that his brother was too eager for this solution, too eager to meet whatever it was on the other side of that shutter. 'Wouldn't we be better staying here?' he said. His arm was heavy in its sling, his pain weighing on it, pulling it down, stretching the sling, dragging at his neck.

'It's not safe,' their father said. 'We can't be sure where the deads are.'

'Won't the outsiders be back soon?'

'They're late. That's why I want to go out there, try to find them, bring them back, but...'

'But?' Sean asked.

'The flies,' the father said. 'If the flies have taken so many of us here in the Villas, then I don't imagine any of the party have survived out there. We have to assume the bell is something to do with them; too much of a coincidence not to be. That means there will be more flies where they're going. We're on our own.'

'But we've got animals and shelter and...' Michael's voice trailed away.

'The Villas were a cooperative,' their father said. Michael knew that their father was persuading himself, going over arguments in his head, talking to himself more than to them. He wanted them to leave the Villas. 'Each of us had a specific job to keep the place going. We could always deal with one or two infections, one or two houses that needed clearing. There were people for that job as well.'

'You,' said Sean.

Their father nodded.

'Then why can't you clear all the houses?' Michael asked. He couldn't understand their father's desire to leave.

'It's too dangerous. There's no support. We never deal with deads on our own.' Except for the Lansdowns, Michael silently added. 'One false step and you two are on your own. I can't risk that. Not now...' This time their father's voice trailed away. He was looking at Michael, at his arm in its sling. The red dots had bled through again.

'I could help,' said Michael. 'You said I was going to be chosen as an outsider.' Their father was shaking his head, lifting his eyes away from Michael's arm and into meeting his eyes, imploring him to stop. But Michael plunged on. 'The brain, right? Get them in the brain and they fall down proper-dead. I only need one hand to hold an axe.'

'No,' their father said.

'We should use the warehouse,' said Sean.

Their father ignored him. 'Mike, you weren't ready yet. When you've grown another six inches you will be. But right now, the deads are all taller than you; you can't reach up with an axe. Another six inches. That's when you'd have been chosen.'

'But you told me I was ready now.'

'I only meant to make you feel better. Like a man.'

'That's stupid!' Michael's pain growled as he exclaimed. 'Why would being a man make me feel better?'

'I thought it helped. You seemed pleased at the time.'

Michael stopped. Their father was right, he had felt better. What more did a boy want except to be a man?

The three of them fell silent. Michael nursed his arm, breathed through the rising pain, felt it, accepted it, let it move through him. Their father watched him.

'You see?' he said, pride swelling his whisper to fill the roof space. 'You're getting to be in control of it. That's bravery, that's strength.' He stopped abruptly. Michael was sure that he had been about to say that he had taught him this control, that he had raised him to be this strong, this brave. He was going to say that he wasn't a little man anymore; he was a real man. He was going to say it because that was what Michael wanted to hear.

Pain thrashed, churning Michael's blood, burning his body, making him grimace and call out in pain. Their father pulled back in shock, as if Michael had spat at him. Sean reached out to his brother, held on to Michael's shoulder as if he could syphon away the pain and the heat.

'No!' Michael hissed. Sean flinched his hand away and Michael turned to him, nodded, showed him it was okay, that it wasn't him. It was their father. 'No, don't say that. I'm not in control.' He stopped as a fresh assault from his pain proved his words. His face was pale and wet in the torchlight, fresh tears streaked his filthy cheeks.

'You are!' their father hissed. 'You're strong, Michael!'

Michael shook his head.

'He's right,' said Sean. 'You are strong. The strongest.' Their father nodded approvingly to Sean. Sean ignored him. 'But not how he says. You're strong like you. You're strong because you're here, because you help me, because you protect me from...' Even as he flashed a look of bitterness at their father, Sean couldn't say it.

Michael smiled at his brother, ignored their father's face and the look of anger and embarrassment that flashed across his features. His pain slowed, calming again, kneading its claws like a cat settling into his lap, but not quite ready to put its claws away yet. 'I'm not a man,' he said to their father. 'And I don't know that I ever will be. Not yet.' Their father started to argue but Michael spoke over him. 'But if I do, I won't be any braver or stronger than I need to be.'

'You don't know,' their father said. He shook his head. 'You don't know.'

'You don't show us. You don't teach us anything,' said Sean. Michael nodded.

'That's not true. You need to know how to survive. You need to be strong. Little men. There's no time for you to be boys. You don't understand that. You don't see what I see, what I've seen.' Their father paused, drew in a deep breath. 'Done the things I've done.'

The boys stared at their father. Memories of their mother flooded Michael's mind. He looked to Sean; could he remember her? Or was he only thinking of the thing behind the shutter?

Their father pulled back from the torch's light, falling into the shadows, rubbing at his face with the heels of his palms. 'You don't know!' he shouted from the darkness.

The boys shrank from him. Sean slipped, his foot shooting out, and he kicked the torch over. It clattered and span, spewing its shaft of light across the tiles and boards, across them, flashing as if they were on a dancefloor in a nightclub, their mother beckoning to them to come dance with her.

It stopped, the beam pointing between Michael and their father, just catching Michael's knees as it made a cone along the dusty boards.

Their father grabbed it, shone it into their eyes, dazzled them. 'Come on,' he said, his words clipped, his voice terse. 'We try to the warehouse.'

In silence, they struggled back into their packs and made their way back through the roof space to their own house. At the top of their ladder, they once again shed their packs, still in silence. Michael didn't bother to protest again and this was Sean's idea, so he stayed quiet too.

'You first, Sean,' their father said, his whispers echoing. 'I'll pass you the bags down.' Once the bags were down, their father helped Michael on the ladder, holding his tightly, securely, helping him keep his balance until he was halfway down, then letting him descend the rest on his own. Michael looked up at their father. He turned away quickly, unable to look into the cold, hard stare fixed on his face.

'We should wait until morning,' Michael said once they were all on the landing and their father had folded the ladder and closed the hatch.

Sean nodded but their father's impatience was clear. He started to say something. The boys watched him bite whatever it was back. He turned on them and made his way to his own bedroom.

That night, as the boys lay in their beds, Sean whispered to Michael, 'It's not fair. He can't be all we have.'

The next day they stood at the warehouse door, Sean a turtle and their father with packs strapped front and back again. Michael cradled his arm in its sling. Their father had changed his bandages that morning and the fresh white poked its nose from his hand. He'd been sullen throughout the process, barely speaking, breath reeking, eyes dark and wet. Michael thought that he hadn't slept at all, tried to imagine the visions that must swim in his head as he tried to sleep. He had asked their father if there was a plan. He'd ignored him, focused on the bandages, and Michael hadn't pushed it.

The sun rose above the roofs of the Villas, but the small party was shaded, their shoes scuffing the dust of the path. 'Is there a plan?' Their father ignored him.

'Dad?' Sean said, 'what are we doing? Where are we going?'

Their father pushed open the door and stepped into the warehouse, the boys trailing after him.

Everything was the wrong way around. Michael and Sean would come here after their chores and the games, the sun would be in the west, beaming through the skylights, casting shadows to the east. Now, the opposite, and the space felt wrong, as if the sun was sneaking behind them, spying on them.

Instinctively, Sean reached out to his favourite roll of carpet, wanting the softness and the warmth. His fingers flinched from the cold, rough material.

At the shutter, Sean stayed quiet while their father fiddled with his keys. Michael watched his fingers fumble, listened to the frustration in his breathing, his constant annoyance baring its life, its teeth through a nasal pulse.

'Dad?' said Michael. 'Dad?' Their father stopped fumbling with the keys and turned on him, glowering down at him, his eyes hooded by heavy brows, his pursed lips almost hidden in a week's growth of beard. Michael staggered a half-step back, then planted his feet, stared up at their father. 'Where are we going?' for long moments, their father continued to glare. Michael thought that he wouldn't answer, that he would only tell him to be quiet, that he might lash out with the back of his hand. He stopped himself from stepping back, pushed his chest forward, the nose of his bandaged arm defiant.

Finally, their father spoke. His voice was rough and he had to cough to make it clearer. He sounded sad. 'There's a leisure centre a half-mile away. There's a group there. We'll go for help; come back; get the animals.'

The boys stared at their father. 'But you said we shouldn't trust other survivors,' said Michael.

'We've no choice,' their father said. He turned back to his keys.

Only the noise of the keys broke the silence that surrounded them. Michael didn't know what to do; their father was lying to them.

'You've never spoken about this group before,' he said, focused on the keys in his dirty hands. 'How long have you known about them?'

Their father exhaled loudly through his nose. 'For a long time,' he snapped. 'We've traded with them before.'

'Traded what?'

Their father forgot the keys, shook his head, his annoyance loud in his nose. He looked straight ahead into the metal of the shutter. Michael could see that he was thinking of an answer, deciding whether to give the information or simply tell Michael to be quiet. 'Foods and medicines,' he said, finally. Michael looked to Sean but his little brother was staring at the keys. Michael could see the eager anticipation pulling him forward, almost making him snatch at the keys. Seemingly satisfied at last, their father selected one of the keys, moved it towards the control panel.

'Dad,' said Michael, 'be careful; there's something on the other side of the shutter.'

'What thing?' their father asked. Michael could hear the indifference in his voice, like he was asking only because he felt he should.

Sean stared at his brother, the betrayal he felt painted onto his face. 'It's nothing!' he snapped. 'There's nothing there.'

Their father looked at each of them in turn. Red lines fissured his eyeballs.

'A thing, a monster.' said Michael 'It knocks at the shutter.'

'He's lying!' Sean shouted. Their father was astonished.

'What are you both talking about?' he demanded.

'It must be one of those things,' said Michael. 'Like Mrs Lansdown.'

Their father shrugged out of his packs, placing both to the side of the shutter. He took his axe from the side strapping and gripped it in his right hand while he inserted and turned the key with his left.

'No!' Sean called out. He moved to hold their father's forearm, tried to keep the axe at his side but the father simply shrugged him away.

'Raise it,' their father said to Michael.

Michael pressed the button and the shutter clattered into life, a fissure of sunlight blinking into existence and then expanding, the shutter lurching up as if it would leap into the air, then slowing and rolling upwards, a torture of screaming and snapping.

Michael saw the thing's booted feet. They were dark and ragged and filthy, their shadow lengthening as the shutter rose. 'Dad,' he warned. Their father just nodded. He was calm now, ready. This was him. This was what he did. The brain. Always the brain. Somehow, Michael knew that their father always got the brain. He saw his mother in the video, saw her eyes turn yellow, saw her beckoning hands turn to reaching claws, saw her skull cleaved in two, an axe buried in her head, saw the hand that held it. He saw it again now, gripping the axe, waiting for the shutter to rise. Michael saw the drinking and the laptop videos and the loneliness and the bitterness. He saw their father having to look into their faces and see their mother every day.

Sean tried to grab at their father again and again he was shrugged off. Michael watched, saw the indifference in their father. The brain, not the heart. Their father pushed Sean away.

'Sean,' Michael called. 'Don't.'

Sean turned on his brother. Hate and betrayal filled his eyes. Michael was burned by it.

Sean hissed like a cat and ducked under the rising shutter, dashing through to the booted feet.

'No!' Michael yelled. He ran at the shutter, ducking beneath it, his pain driving him on. For a second he was blinded by the sunlight. Then, silhouettes took shape; Sean was already on his backside, scuttling away from the dead as it towered over him, arms raised, head down. Then it was leaning, toppling to its knees, reaching for Sean. Michael slammed into it with his shoulder, sending it tumbling to the side. He crashed down on top of it, crushing his arm, making his pain scream through his body. He'd started to roll away, but he was dizzied by that scream, confused, and he lolled on the dead like an overturned turtle.

'Mike!' Sean was screaming his name. The shutters were screaming their ascent. His pain was screaming through his body.

The dead's hands clutched at his sides, squeezing and scrabbling at his t-shirt and his flesh. Its hands were on his belly, pulling and squeezing. He could feel its head beneath his, turning against the weight of his skull. He jerked his own head up as it snapped its teeth, his hair clamped in its mouth, pulling at his scalp. He felt no pain from that or from the fingers digging at his belly. There was just one pain; nothing about his body was specific, it was one mass of pain, of fire, burning as if his body were his coffin in an incinerator and he was trapped inside, thrashing impotently in the growing heat.

'Mike!'

Sean was near him; he couldn't understand where; it was all he could do to hold his head up, away from the dead's snapping teeth. Sean was scrambling at his side, reaching under him, grabbing at the dead.

'Dad!' Sean was yelling at their father. Michael could hear his brother's voice as if he were shouting from a great distance, as if he were calling down to the ally from behind a closed back-bedroom window.

'Dad!' Sean yelled and yelled. Michael could feel him holding the dead as still as he could. His voice was clearer now, nearer, almost as near as his mouth which must only be an arm's length from his ear. Closer! He could feel Sean's elbows rubbing bumping at the side of his head. He could feel individual pains, the thing's fingers in his belly, its teeth pulling at his hair.

'Dad!' Sean yelled. 'Please!'

Michael rose above the pain, pulling his head out of the fire. Sean was next to him, his face red with the struggle of holding the dead, and beyond him was their father. The open shutter was just above his head. He stared at them, the axe limp at his side. Michael froze, his pain watching with him, as he met their father's eyes. Nothing. There was nothing there. Their father had left.

Anger pushed at his pain, forced it back. Michael grabbed at the dead's hands, pulled at the fingers that were trying to dig into his belly. He could feel the thing's bones just beneath its papery skin; he couldn't believe the strength in something so frail. With just one hand, he couldn't drag the dead's hands away no matter how hard he pulled at them.

'Mike!' Sean was shouting.

Michael did not have the breath to answer. He made a desperate grab at one of the thing's fingers, curling it into his fist. He pulled. It snapped. Michael let go, horrified at the feeling. The finger wavered uselessly above his belly. Michael grabbed the next finger, pulled and snapped, the next, the next, pulling and snapping, the pain at his belly receding, the grip on his body loosening. Finally, the dead had too few fingers to hold him, and he rolled away, trying to protect his arm, yelling at his pain, daring it to try to hold him back.

Dizzied again, stars floating in his vision, bile rising in his throat, Michael's vision blurred as he watched Sean let go of the dead's ears and scramble away on his backside.

Now the dead was the upturned turtle. Its limbs poked into the air, its fingers limp. Michael quashed his pain again, and his vision cleared. He nodded his thanks to Sean but his younger brother was staring at the dead, tears rolling freely down his cheeks.

It wasn't their mother.

It was, it had been, a man. Fat and bloated around its torso, its limbs skinny and angular, a ridiculous and deadly toad. Its once-fat face, framed by dark, filthy, tangled hair, had had a beard, but it was torn away in places along with its cheeks, the skin flapping open, drool dripping and reddened by what little blood still leaked from its mouth. The rest of its face was caked in black, flaking blood, its eyes yellow pits, staring at nothing, yet alive with hunger.

It moved more purposefully, rolling onto its side, holding Michael's gaze every centimetre of the way. It was on its hands and knees, crawling towards him, its snarling, flapping mouth freezing him. On the other side of it, Sean was similarly frozen, only his tears moving. Why me? Michael thought. A bolt of pain from, his arm made him look down, and he saw the fresh blood seeping through his bandages. The dead was drawn to it, reaching for his bloody stump, its broken fingers bending uselessly against it. Michael drew back; the thing's hands fell onto his shins. He could feel it trying to grab at him with its few functioning fingers. He kicked at it, whipping his feet at the hands, shuffling back as he flailed. He backed into their father's legs, tried to push him back but he may as well have tried to push against a brick wall. He looked up. Their father looked down at him, his eyes still dark, still blank, uncaring.

'Dad!' Michael yelled. The dead was on his legs, crawling forward, unable to grip Michael's flesh or clothes, but its face, its snapping teeth, were ever closer.

Michael's wild stare switched between the dead and their father. He pushed back as hard as he could. Their father stumbled, just a little. Michael raised his arms into the air, the fingers of his hand spread and pleading, the bloody bandages of his stump waving right below their father's face. The dead came on, its head raised as it followed the blood, its eyes forgetting Michael and jerking back and forth, up and down, hypnotised by the blood, it's teeth just centimetres from his face

Something woke their father. His eyes gained focus, watched the blood-soaked bandage. He started, raised the axe automatically, chopping it into the dead's head, splattering Michael in blood and bone and brain.

Their father was on one knee, pulling the dead away from Michael, allowing Michael to roll away and vomit onto the tiled floor. He wretched over and over, the dead's blood and brains dripping down his face.

'Mike!' Sean was with him again. 'Mike, are you okay?' His little brother worried at his shoulders and back.

Their father was there, smoothing Michael's hair back from his forehead.

'Get away!' Sean shouted. 'Get away from him!' He pushed at their father, shoving at his arms, his chest. Their father was unmoved. He ignored Sean, focused on Michael.

'I'm sorry,' their father said. 'I'm sorry.' He said it over and over. 'I'm sorry.'

Michael gasped over the puddle of vomit, their father's words at the edge of his hearing. It was Sean he finally turned to. 'I'm okay,' he said. He reached out to his shoulder, wanted him to stop shouting at their father, tried to soothe him. 'It's okay. I'm okay.'

Slowly, Michael turned to their father. His wide eyes were red, there were tears falling into his beard. He looked away, unable to meet his son's eyes and he sobbed as his face fell.

'I'm so sorry,' their father said.

'You were going to let us die,' said Sean.

Their father raised his eyes to look at him, starting to shake his head, but stopped, slumped, his shoulders falling as if some string that had been holding him was cut.

'Bastard!' Sean spat at him. 'You bastard!'

Michael watched their father cry. He felt nothing, no anger or pity or shame, no hate, no forgiveness. He wiped at his face, scraping the filth away. His breathing steadied, his nausea calmed, his pain retreated. 'Is that why you wanted us to leave?' he asked their father. Michael didn't want to hear the answer. Their father had pushed them into an 'accident'. Now, he simply sagged, a pile of shame wilting in the morning sun that flooded through the carpet shop's windows.

'Bastard,' Sean hissed again.

Michael looked to his brother. The sun was behind him, leaving his face dark and his eyes flashing from the shadows, wide with hate and betrayal. Then he was on his feet and Michael thought he would attack their father, but he turned on his heels, walked to the sunlit windows, squaring his shoulders against their father's eyes as he walked away.

'He shouldn't...' their father started but fell silent.

'Shouldn't what?' Michael asked.

'Walk off alone. It's always dangerous outside the Villas.'

'There's nothing out there,' Sean called over from the window. 'Just an empty, dirty street.'

Michael struggled to his feet, went to join his brother. He stared out into the sunlit street. Sean was right; it was just an empty, dirty street. But it was different. A new view, something he'd not seen every day for five years. He stared at streetlights, a parked car, rusted and sagging on its flat tyres, black dust from the year-long night, windows, some smashed, all filthy. Some of the gutters dangled greenery, some of the houses had ivy trying to smother them, some of the front gardens had bushes and once-small trees spilling out onto the footpaths. The road was cracked and more greenery was poking through. A dog ran past.

'Look!' Sean shouted.

'A dog!' said Michael, excited. He started to turn to their father, to tell him about the dog, then he remembered, and turned back to the window.

It was wonderful.

To their left the front door. A pane of glass between them and the outside world. To their right another door, this time to an office. There was a window next to it with the blinds lowered about two-thirds.

'There's no smell,' said Michael. 'It's clear.'

Sean looked up at him, then at the mess of the dead on the floor. 'It smells bad in here,' he said.

'Out there,' said Michael, gesturing at the window. He raised his face to a crack in the glass. 'There's no smell out there.' Sean eyed him dubiously.

Their father was with them, standing between them and the office. He saw them looking between the window and the door to their left, the exit. 'It's too dangerous,' he said.

Michael didn't say that their father had been about to take them out there. Neither did Sean. Neither of them looked at their father. Both took a step away from him towards the door.

'There are no deads out there,' said Michael.

'There are always deads,' their father said. 'Always.'

The boys moved another step away from him. 'The bell,' said Michael. 'They'll all have gone towards the bell. You knew that. You knew that we'd be okay if we went out there.' Michael knew he was speaking too quickly, too desperately, but he plunged on. 'You knew! Say you knew!'

'He didn't,' said Sean.

'You must have known!'

Their father shrank from Michael's shout, stepped back, half-raised his hands to protest but said nothing, couldn't say anything. Behind him, the blind at the window to the office moved. Michael saw it clearly.

'What's that?' Michael asked. He gestured to the window. Their father turned. Sean glared at the back of his head.

'There's always more deads,' their father said. 'Stay back.' He moved to the office door. The boys couldn't help but shuffle forward.

The blind moved again, and something else, something below the blind. It was a rush of colour, of a flowered print pressed against the glass of the office window. A dress.

Sean gasped. Michael couldn't stop him as he rushed forward just as their father was opening the door, raising his axe, readying himself to chop into the dead's head.

'No, it's Mum!' Sean shouted. He crashed into their father, who looked down at Sean in astonishment. Their father stumbled, falling into the dead. Michael could see it now; it was a woman, slim, pale, haggard. Not their mother, hardly like her at all. It fell with their father's weight on top of it, crashing against a desk, the two of them flipping over, their father hitting the floor first, the dead falling onto him, gnashing its teeth at his face. He tried to raise his hands, tried to push at it with his knees. Too late, the thing had bitten into his face, chewing into his cheek below his left eye. He screamed and thrashed his legs, dropped the axe, lashed at the dead with hands and arms. It hung on like a fish caught on a line, flopping as their father spasmed beneath it, but it had its arms around him, clamping him against it, chewing into his face over and over, pulling and tearing at the skin on the left side of his head. Blood spilled and splashed, flicking across his shoulder, across his head, across the dead's face and jaw.

The boys stared, frozen by shock and horror. The smell of iron, the noise of their father's screams, the triumphant grunts and snorts of the dead.

'Mum?' said Sean. 'Mum, don't.'

'It's not Mum,' said Michael. 'It can't be Mum.' He stepped forward, grabbed the axe. Their father saw him, his screaming quietened, he was nodding to Michael. Michael raised the axe. It was heavier than he had imagined. He swung it into the back of the dead's head. It didn't stop. Michael had held back, he knew. The thought of chopping into a person's head, of killing, pulling his swing. He turned to Sean, half expecting, half hoping his brother to try to stop him, but Sean was still frozen, staring at the dead as it attacked their father. Michael retightened his grip on the handle, wished he had two hands to swing it harder, raised the axe and brought it down as hard as could. He felt the blade bite into the thing's skull and embed itself. As it flopped down on their father, the handle was jerked from his hand.

He stepped back to Sean, wanting to hold his hand, wanting to run away, back into the Villas, into the alley and pretend it had all been a game, and now they had work to do; the pigs and the chickens needed feeding. Someone had to watch for angels, raise the birdsong to warn the Villas.

But this was real, loudly and painfully real. The smell of the thing, that smell that had been part of his life for five years, filled his nostrils. Their father still moved, still panted and shouted in pain as he pushed the body of the dead away. Michael turned from their father's torn, bloody face, suddenly nauseous again.

Sean stepped closer. 'Get up,' he said. Their father didn't. Couldn't. 'Get up!' Sean demanded. 'You can't leave us. You can't do this to us and then leave us!'

Their father was shaking his head, his agonised breathing rasping through his tattered cheeks. He raised his hands, one to each of his boys. Neither went to him.

Slowly, his arms lowered, his hands flopping weakly on the floor.

Michael stepped forward, past Sean, and leaned over their father. He looked right into his eyes. Their father gasped, blood bubbling at his lips and in the rents in his face. 'The brain,' said Michael. 'I'll get the brain.' He stooped to pull the axe from the dead woman's head. 'Do you want me to wait?' Their father shook his head.

Author's note

Thanks for reading!

There are more stories set in this bleak apocalyptic world. Stella the Zombie Killer is a series of novels that track Stella's fight for survival in a dead-infested London.

Reviews for Stella the Zombie Killer:

"I bought a copy of Stella on the strength of "Suspended" by the same author. I had enjoyed "Suspended" and liked the style it was written in. Little did I know this was totally different! Very quickly I was in deep and running for survival with the main characters. A futuristic world populated by zombies. I don't believe in spoiling a great story by giving anything away here. It's enough for me to say you need to read this book. I am waiting for book two to answer questions I have and can't wait to be reunited with "Stella". Great job Mr. Wilkinson. Please let your fans know when we can have the next dose of Stella!"

"Fast paced, easy, addictive reading. Wonderful atmospheric illustrations."

"The quality of this first volume lies in how Alistair manages to give the reader so much from such a small cache of characters and settings. We see webs of connectivity attach and interweave in a pacey yet completely organic fashion. The claustrophobic ambience that is draped over almost the entire book never allows the reader to get too settled for too long; there is always something around the corner and the corner is always too close for comfort to begin with! We have been given crumbs of the wider horizon that is clearly enveloping London and the small crew in the museum and I can't wait to read the other books to find out more!"

"Stella is gory, funny, touching, realistic, brutal... all that you would hope for from this type of book, but, what sets it apart from its contemporaries is that it's brilliantly, beautifully written. The prose is detailed, flowing, lovingly crafted; it transports you into Stella's brutal London of the future and immerses you in its characters' desperate struggle not just for survival, but to cling on to the vestiges of their humanity."

"Stella is a kick-ass yet vulnerable character brought to high tech augmented life by the brilliant writer Alistair Wilkinson in a fast-paced, exciting and often gory story set in post-apocalyptic London. Three years after it all kicks off, we see Stella and her band of survivors making their way through the deads, the sorrows and the hardships of life without the iPhone! However, the scariest encounters in this world of horror are not necessarily with the shambling, rotting, teeth-gnashing deads; there are very human monsters lurking in the shadows, less than angelic angels and heart-stopping surprises around every corner. The book also contains some really stunning artwork by the talented artist Alison Rasmussen. This is an unputdownable read with humour as well as page-turning suspense and horror - if you like The Walking Dead, Stephen King or just a ripping yarn, you should definitely treat yourself to a bit of Stella. Can't wait for Volume Two!"

"This has all the action-packed tension that you want from a zombie apocalypse, but Alistair Wilkinson's dystopian future is also original and intriguing, and his characters conflict-ridden and compelling. Amidst the fight for survival there's betrayal, hope, revenge, love and mystery. I liked Suspended, but Stella was even better, I was hooked from start to finish. Consistently entertaining, dramatic and fun. Can't wait to get stuck into the sequel..."

Reviews for Of Deads:

"This book is a brutal journey into a nihilistic world. The writing is masterful, and the plot leaves you breathless. Fast-paced and terrifying, it leaves you fearing no one is safe. This writer can really construct a line, a paragraph, a chapter, an alternative reality. All whilst making the reader feel as if everything just might fall apart. Amazing!"

"Alistair Wilkinson is a skilled storyteller and Of Deads is a non-stop trip. The descriptions of the panic and chaos which ensues following the big event in the story are vivid and completely absorbing; the characters are so well written that it's hard not to care about their fates. The setting really makes the story - choosing the iconic bridge to be centre stage was a genius move! Full disclosure - I'm already a big fan of the 'Stella' series, so I was really excited about this coming out, but it's also a good starting point for anyone who hasn't visited Stella's world yet. I'd really recommend to anyone who likes dystopia, adventure, or just enjoys a ripping yarn!"

"Alistair captures the grim unreality of an uncertain future. I've read many apocalyptic horror novels and sometimes find that the plot is usually superior to the writing. In Alistair's case the craft is superb, this man can certainly write!

Of Deads is not for the faint hearted, but the characters are well rounded and realistically portray the traumas and reactions of normal people in abnormal situations.

I read this book in a single day. The book made that easy though, it flowed well and time had passed until I realised that I was nearing the end."

"One of my favourite series ever and this prequel doesn't disappoint. The characters are carefully drawn, the action compelling, and the misery and suspense of the zombie genre permeates the book leaving you dreading the next event as much as anticipating it. Do yourself a favour and read this and then the whole series - you won't regret it."

Acknowledgements

As always, I've been so lucky to have so much help putting this book together. 'Of Deads' is different to my other books and so my regular proof-readers have been challenged to read this nihilistic tale without the relief of the high-kicking, hard-punching, harsh-punning Stella. Of course, they were all stars and saw me through to the end, and another end, and another end... In no particular order, I need to thank my dad, Lucy Adams, Sue Firth, Natalie Smith, and Duncan Cook (who again read it all in one sitting!). And to Chris Lillywhite for fabulous cover art and for putting up with my constant requests for 'tiny' alterations. And Alison Rasmussen for all the hours of toil that have brought the world of Stella the Zombie Killer to life. As always, I couldn't do any of this without you.

Thank you to you all.

Remember, the Cynosure fights for you.

Printed in Great Britain
by Amazon